THE SLAVE-GIRL
FROM JERUSALEM

THE ROMAN MYSTERIES
by Caroline Lawrence

And look out for:

A Roman Mystery

THE SLAVE-GIRL FROM JERUSALEM

Caroline Lawrence

Orion
Children's Books

First published in Great Britain in 2007
by Orion Children's Books
a division of the Orion Publishing Group Ltd
Orion House
5 Upper St Martin's Lane
London WC2H 9EA

A catalogue record for this book is
available from the British Library

ISBN 978 1 84255 188 2

Typeset at The Spartan Press Ltd,
Lymington, Hants

Printed in Great Britain by
Clays Ltd, St Ives plc

The Orion Publishing Group's policy is to use papers that
are natural, renewable and recyclable products and made
from wood grown in sustainable forests. The logging and
manufacturing processes are expected to conform to the
environmental regulations of the country of origin.

www.orionbooks.co.uk

To the cast and crew of the Roman Mysteries
TV series . . . with sincere apologies to those
whose characters I have had to kill

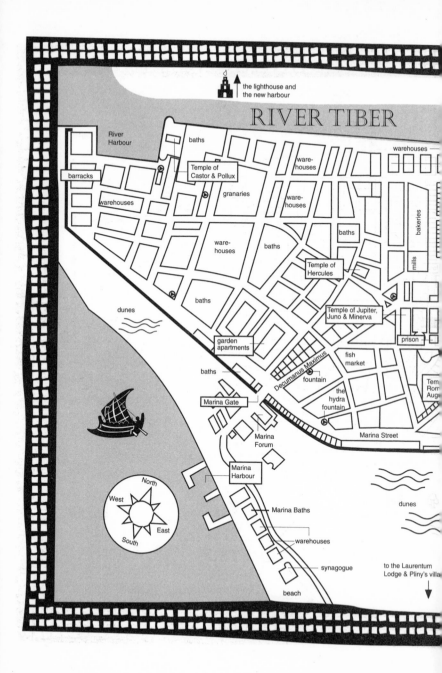

the lighthouse and
the new harbour

RIVER TIBER

River Harbour

baths

warehouses

Temple of Castor & Pollux

barracks

granaries

warehouses

ware-houses

ware-houses

bakeries

mills

baths

ware-houses

baths

Temple of Hercules

dunes

baths

Temple of Jupiter, Juno & Minerva

prison

garden apartments

fish market

baths

Decumanus Maximus

fountain

Marina Gate

the hydra fountain

Tem Rom Aug

Marina Forum

Marina Street

Marina Harbour

North

West

East

South

Marina Baths

dunes

warehouses

synagogue

to the Laurentum
Lodge & Pliny's villa

beach

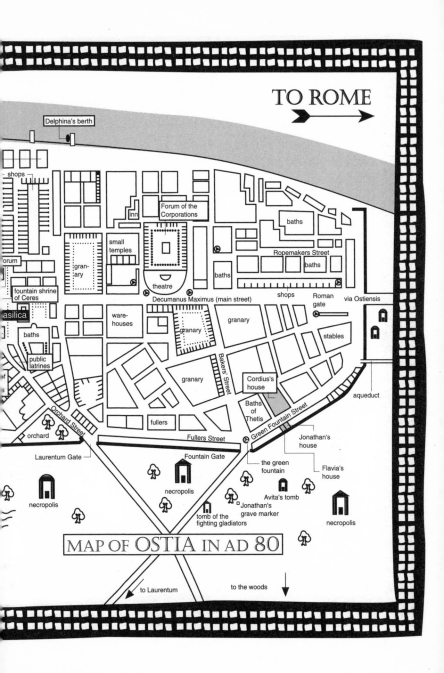

TO ROME

Delphina's berth

shops

Forum of the Corporations

inn

small temples

granary

fountain shrine of Ceres

orum

basilica

baths

public latrines

theatre

Decumanus Maximus (main street)

ware-houses

granary

granary

granary

baths

Ropemakers Street

baths

shops

Roman gate

via Ostiensis

stables

Bakers' Street

Cordius's house

Baths of Thetis

fullers

Orchard Street

orchard

Laurentum Gate

Fullers Street

Green Fountain Street

aqueduct

Jonathan's house

Flavia's house

Fountain Gate

the green fountain

necropolis

necropolis

Avita's tomb

Jonathan's grave marker

tomb of the fighting gladiators

necropolis

MAP OF OSTIA IN AD 80

to Laurentum

to the woods

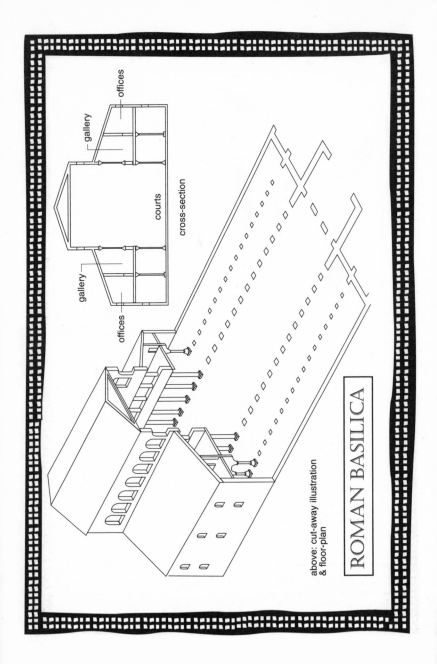

gallery

offices

courts

gallery

offices

cross-section

above: cut-away illustration
& floor-plan

ROMAN BASILICA

below left: the classic gesture for silence

above: the gesture for declamation, narration or 'wait a moment'

above: gesture suitable for the exordium

above: gesture expressing amazement or wonder

above: the gesture for 'perfect' or 'excellent'

THE ORATOR'S GESTURES

This story takes place in ancient Roman times, so a few of the words may look strange.

If you don't know them, 'Aristo's Scroll' at the back of the book will tell you what they mean and how to pronounce them. It will also explain some of the Roman legal terms mentioned in this story.

At the beginning of this book are illustrations of some of the gestures used by Roman orators in the first century AD.

SCROLL I

Someone was going to die; of that he was perfectly sure.

The only question was who.

Jonathan ben Mordecai had suffered from premonitions once before in his life. It had happened the previous year, when he was eleven. He and his father and sister Miriam had been staying with friends near a mountain called Vesuvius. He had dreamt of disaster, and disaster had come with the mountain's eruption.

Now, back in Rome's port of Ostia, another dream had begun to haunt him. In this dream, mourners carried a body on a bier through the foggy streets of the city.

Jonathan shivered and put up the hood of his nutmeg-coloured cloak. It was the first Sabbath of December, cold and foggy, just as it always was in his dream. He had been up since dawn, hunting outside the town walls with his dog Tigris. He stroked the soft rabbits that hung limply from his belt. He had been hoping for more than two, but it was unlikely that he would catch any this late in the morning, so he whistled for his dog, and set back through the dripping umbrella pines, heading for the Fountain Gate.

Tigris came up from behind, then forged ahead, a

dark shape weaving through the long damp grasses with his head down. Suddenly he stopped, tested the air with his nose, and turned in the direction of the sea. He whined.

'What is it, boy? Do you smell another rabbit?' Jonathan sniffed, too. The distinctive pork-sweet odour of burning human flesh raised the little hairs on his arms. 'A funeral pyre,' he muttered, and shivered again. 'Shall we go and investigate?'

They set off together in the direction of the sea, skirting a copse of dripping green acacia trees and then passing through umbrella pines, some so tall that their dark green canopies were swallowed by the mist.

Emerging into the fog-shrouded dunes, he saw the bright flames of a funeral pyre surrounded by forty or fifty mourners, dark shapes in the mist. As he drew closer, he saw that most of them were dressed in black, but a dozen or so wore the colourful, conical hats of freedmen.

'It must have been someone rich,' said Jonathan to Tigris. 'He probably freed some slaves in his will.'

A stout woman in a grey palla was standing a little apart from the other mourners. Jonathan walked over to her.

'Who was it?' he asked.

The woman turned a genial, weather-beaten face towards him. 'Gaius Artorius Dives,' she said, 'owned an estate down the road near Laurentum.' She jerked her thumb to the south.

'Dives? Was he rich?'

'Very.' She chuckled. 'Clever, too. He deceived all his captators.'

'Captators?'

2

'You know. Legacy-hunters. Men and women who hang around the sick and dying, hoping for a mention in the will.'

'Ah. So he didn't have a wife or children, then.'

'Nor brother, nor uncle, nor cousin.' She chuckled again and said, 'He kept the captators dangling like fishies on the rod. And then he left them nothing. Well, five sesterces each.'

'Five hundred sesterces each? That's not bad.'

'Not five hundred. Five.'

Jonathan's eyebrows went up. 'That sounds more like an insult than a legacy.'

'It was.' She winked. 'As the saying goes: *Romans tell the truth but once in their lives, when writing their wills.*'

'Did he leave *you* anything in his will?'

She nodded happily. 'He granted me my freedom and a few hundred sesterces. That's my new patron: Lucius Nonius Celer.' She pointed with her chin to a swarthy young man standing close to the pyre. 'Dives made him his heir. Left him the lot. Now he's the rich one.'

'This boy's not bothering you, is he, Restituta?' said a voice behind them. Jonathan turned to see a small, middle-aged man with a dark beard and a white skull-cap.

'Oh, no,' chuckled Restituta. 'We were just talking about poor old Dives.'

'Don't I know you?' said the man, with a smile. 'Didn't you used to attend the synagogue?'

'Yes,' said Jonathan.

'Oh, so you're one of us,' said the woman.

Jonathan nodded.

3

'Why don't I see you there anymore?' asked the man. 'At the synagogue, I mean.'

Jonathan considered telling them that his father – Mordecai ben Ezra – followed a new sect called The Way, and that because of this they had been banned from the synagogue and rejected by the Jewish community, even by his father's relatives. Before he could think how to phrase this, the woman came to his rescue.

'Not really any of your business, is it, Gaius?' she said cheerfully.

'No, I suppose not.' The man winked at Jonathan. 'My name's Staphylus,' he added. 'Gaius Artorius Staphylus.'

'You have the same first names as Gaius Artorius Dives,' said Jonathan, looking at the pyre, 'which means he freed you, too. Mazal tov!'

Staphylus chuckled. 'That's right. But I'm not one of the new batch like Artoria Restituta here. Old Dives freed me a few years ago when he made me his chief bailiff. It's a nice estate. I enjoy managing it. Cattle, vines, olives, and the best mulberry grove in Italia.' He jerked his chin at the swarthy young man who stood by the pyre. 'I just hope young Nonius over there gives me as much free reign in running the estate as Dives did.'

'And I hope he'll be as friendly to us Jews,' said the woman. 'Another thing I can tell you about Dives, now that I know you're one of us: he was a righteous gentile. He bought lots of Jewish slaves but I reckon he did it to treat us well. Never beat us or nothing.'

'Didn't stop him having his funeral on the Sabbath,' grumbled Staphylus.

'Don't suppose he had a choice about that,' chuckled the woman. 'Anyway, it was his heir's decision.'

Staphylus looked at the rabbits hanging from Jonathan's belt. 'Is that why you don't attend our services? To hunt non-kosher game on the Sabbath?'

'Um . . . I'd better be going,' said Jonathan, and whistled for Tigris.

'Now you've gone and frightened him off,' said the woman. 'Told you not to be nosey.'

'It was nice to meet you,' said Jonathan, as Tigris bounded up. 'Shalom, Staphylus. Shalom . . .'

'Restituta,' chuckled the woman. 'Shalom, yourself.'

Jonathan and Tigris started back towards the road which led up to the Fountain Gate. He glanced over his shoulder once to see Staphylus and Restituta watching him, their features already blurred by fog and by smoke from the funeral pyre. They gave him a cheerful wave. He waved back and quickened his pace.

Most of the tombs in Ostia lined the roads into town, but there were also grave markers and altars scattered behind the roads, among the pines.

He crossed the road to Laurentum and had just passed the tomb of fighting gladiators, when something made him stop dead.

It was a cube of stone at the base of an umbrella pine.

He turned back and frowned down at the red letters painted on the white marble. And for the third time that morning he shivered.

'Great Jupiter's eyebrows,' he muttered to Tigris, 'it's my grave.'

'Jonathan!' called a girl's voice. 'Jonathan!'

'Here, Flavia!' he called back. 'I'm over here. Behind the tomb of fighting gladiators!'

'Oh! There you are!' A girl with light brown hair and

a sky-blue palla emerged from the mist-choked umbrella pines. Flavia Gemina was Jonathan's next-door neighbour and friend. Together with their friends Nubia and Lupus, they had solved several mysteries and had many adventures.

Flavia's dog Scuto emerged from the fog behind her. Tigris ran to meet his friend and the two dogs – one black, one gold – gave each other a quick sniff of greeting. Although Tigris was not yet a year and half old, he was already bigger than the fully-grown Scuto.

'We've been looking for you everywhere,' said Flavia breathlessly. 'Nubia went west and I went east, and Lupus is searching the baths.'

Jonathan did not reply. Instead he raised his eyebrows and pointed at the marble block.

Looking down, Flavia read the inscription: '*To the spirits of the underworld, for Jonathan ben Mordecai. His friends Flavia, Nubia and Lupus set this up for him, their well-deserving friend.*' She looked guiltily up at him. 'Oops!' she covered her mouth with her hand.

'Oops, indeed.'

'We were going to tell you, but then we forgot.'

'You forgot to tell me I died?'

'Jonathan! Don't say such a thing!' Flavia made the sign against evil and then spat onto the ground for good measure. 'We put it up last spring, when we thought you were dead. But you weren't dead. You were a gladiator. Remember?'

'If I try very hard,' said Jonathan, 'I *think* I can remember not being dead.'

'You know what I mean.' Flavia's grey eyes were bright with excitement.

He raised an eyebrow at her. 'What's the mystery?'

'What? You – how did you know?'

'You get a certain gleam in your eye.'

She grinned. 'It's your sister Miriam. She's here. I don't mean here in the graveyard. I mean here in Ostia. At your house. And Jonathan, you're right: she has a mystery for us to solve!'

SCROLL II

Flavia thought Miriam was the most beautiful girl she had ever seen.

With her glossy dark curls, huge violet eyes and creamy skin, Jonathan's sister could stop a column of legionaries dead in their tracks. Last month she had actually caused a collision between two mule-carts just inside the Roman Gate; even at eight months pregnant, she was so breathtaking that the drivers had not been able to keep their eyes off her.

Flavia knew that Miriam hated such attention from men. That was why she usually pulled her palla over her head like a modest matron. But here in her father's house she went unveiled. Wearing a dark-blue stola and sitting on the red and orange striped divan, her beauty was ripe and luminous.

Flavia sighed. Miriam was not only beautiful, but she was kind and compassionate. She was also a skilled mid-wife. Even though she herself was heavily pregnant, she still attended the births of poor women and female slaves who could not afford a doctor.

A slave-girl stepped into the dining room doorway. As usual, Flavia tried not to stare: the girl had the name 'Delilah' branded on her forehead. Jonathan's mother, Susannah had brought her back from Rome.

'Excuse me,' said Delilah. 'Nubia is here.'

A dark-skinned girl in a lionskin cloak came into the tablinum, closely followed by a black dog.

'Nubia!' cried Flavia. 'And Nipur! Now that we're all here, Miriam can tell us her mystery.'

'Have a mint tea, Nubia,' said Jonathan, as the dogs greeted one another.

Beside him, a dark-haired boy in a sea-green tunic waved and pointed at a plate of almond-stuffed dates. Lupus was an ex-beggar boy who lived with Jonathan. He had no tongue and could not speak.

'Greetings!' said Nubia, handing her lionskin cloak to Delilah. She took a beaker of mint tea and a handful of dates and sat gracefully beside Flavia.

'Miriam was just telling us about her new friend, Hephzibah,' explained Flavia.

Nubia frowned. 'Hephzibah? That is a name I am never hearing before.' Nubia had been in Italia for a year and a half, but her Latin was not yet fluent.

'It's a Hebrew name,' explained Miriam. 'Hephzibah was born in Jerusalem, just like me. We used to be best friends when we were four years old. Then I met her last month when I was attending a pregnant slave at the estate where she lives. We've become good friends again.'

Flavia turned to Nubia and said through a mouthful of stuffed dates: 'Miriam wants Hephzibah to go live with her and Uncle Gaius. To help when the baby is born.'

On the divan beside Jonathan, Lupus made a slicing motion across his throat, crossed his eyes, and fell back onto the red cushions.

'What Lupus is trying to say,' explained Flavia, 'is that Hephzibah's master died yesterday.'

'Was someone cutting his throat?' asked Nubia.

Lupus shook his head. He shaped an imaginary fat belly and then played dead again.

Jonathan grinned. 'He was pregnant?'

Lupus laughed and grunted no, then puffed out his cheeks and tucked his chin down.

'He died of fatness?' said Nubia.

Lupus gave her a thumbs-up.

'At least that's what his slaves say,' explained Miriam. 'His name was Dives and he owned an estate near us.'

'Dives!' said Jonathan. 'I've just come from his funeral.'

They all stared at him and Jonathan explained, 'I was hunting and I saw them burning his body. The slaves were probably right about his dying of fatness. He made a blazing fire.'

Nubia shuddered but Flavia turned excitedly to Miriam. 'I'll bet I can guess what your mystery is: you suspect Dives was murdered, and you want us to find the killer!'

'Nothing as dramatic as that,' said Miriam. 'I'm sure Dives died a natural death. The mystery is that a few days before he died, Dives set Hephzibah free.'

Nubia looked up from stroking Nipur. 'The man who dies of fatness?' she said. 'He sets your friend free?'

'Yes. But he warned her not to tell anyone what he had done.'

'Why didn't he want her to tell anyone?' asked Flavia.

'I don't know. She doesn't know.'

'She told *you*,' said Jonathan, raising an eyebrow.

'I know.' Miriam's eyes suddenly filled with tears. 'And I wish she'd told more people. That's part of the problem. Dives died a few days after setting Hephzibah free. He left his entire estate to a man called Nonius, but—'

'That's right,' interrupted Jonathan. 'Nonius Celer. He was at the funeral.'

Miriam nodded. 'But Nonius says there's no record of Hephzibah's manumission.'

'What is man you mission?' asked Nubia.

'Manumission,' said Flavia, 'is the act of freeing a slave.'

Miriam continued. 'Nonius – the new owner of the estate – claims that Hephzibah is still his property. If only she'd told some of the other slaves or freedmen, they could confirm her claim. But apart from the man who witnessed the manumission, I was the only one who knew about it.'

'There was a witness?' asked Flavia.

'Apparently,' said Miriam.

'Then surely *he* can testify that your friend was set free?'

'That's the mystery,' said Miriam. 'We can't find the witness anywhere.'

'What's his name?' asked Jonathan.

Miriam shook her head. 'Hephzibah can't remember. She thinks he might be called something like Gaius Helvidius Pupienus. He's some kind of official. If it helps, she described him to me.'

'It helps.' Flavia took out her wax tablet and made a note of the name.

'According to Hephzibah, he has thinning hair, a long nose and a small butterfly-shaped birthmark over his left eyebrow.' Miriam leaned forward: 'Flavia, we need to find him. Hephzibah has summoned her new master to court, and we need the witness to prove she's free.'

'Can she do that?' asked Jonathan. 'Can a slave summon a citizen to court?'

'She can't,' said Miriam. 'But another citizen can.'

'I'll bet it's Uncle Gaius,' said Flavia. 'Has Uncle Gaius agreed to be her protector and take on her case?'

'No,' said Miriam. 'Gaius is terribly busy with the farm. The olive harvest isn't quite in. Also, he doesn't know very much about legal matters.' She lowered her head and stroked her belly. 'So I've asked Gaius Plinius Secundus to help.'

'Pliny!' cried Flavia. 'You asked Pliny?'

'Yes.'

'And he agreed to help your friend?'

'Of course Pliny agreed,' said Jonathan drily. 'He's madly in love with Miriam.'

'Don't be ridiculous, Jonathan,' murmured Miriam, but her head was still down.

Flavia exchanged a knowing look with Nubia. 'It's not that ridiculous, Miriam,' she said. 'Pliny was passionately in love with you last summer.'

Miriam looked up at Flavia. 'But he's not in love with me now,' she replied firmly. 'He is studying rhetoric and said he would welcome a chance to plead a case.'

Jonathan snorted. 'If you say so.'

Delilah appeared in the doorway again. 'Excuse me, but a carriage has arrived. Driver says he goes to Laurentum.'

'That's me,' said Miriam, rising awkwardly to her feet. 'One of Pliny's slaves was running an errand here in Ostia. He brought me in and now he's taking me back.'

Once again her eyes brimmed with tears as she looked at each of them in turn. 'Please. The four of you must find that witness. Hephzibah has no other proof that Dives set her free. Without that witness she can never come to live with us. And she must come to live with us. She must!'

The December sun had burned off the fog and was now high enough to throw a shadow on the new sundial in Flavia's inner garden.

'We have to find that witness,' said Flavia, pacing up and down the garden path, 'and we need to work fast. Miriam said Hephzibah thought he was an official. All the public buildings close at noon. According to this,' she gestured towards the sundial, 'that only gives us half an hour. Any ideas about where we should start looking?'

'How about the basilica?' said Jonathan. 'There's usually a list of officials posted there, and one of the clerks or scribes might know of one with a butterfly birthmark.'

'Excellent!' said Flavia. 'Any other ideas?'

Nubia nodded shyly. 'Aristo is visiting his friend Leander this morning,' she said. 'But he said he would return for lunch before he goes to the baths. I will wait here and ask him.'

'Good. And if pater should appear, you can ask him, too.'

'Where is your father?' asked Jonathan.

'He's gone to Sicily for his patron's wedding. Didn't I

tell you? Cordius is going to marry Avita's mother, Julia Firma!'

'Avita's mother?'

'Yes. You remember Avita. The little girl who died of a mad dog's bite.'

'Of course. I often pass her tomb.'

'And you remember that Avita's father died?'

'How could I forget that?'

'And do you remember how her mother – Julia Firma – was all alone in the world and how Cordius took her in as a seamstress, because she had no means to live? Well, Cupid must have fired an arrow because they're getting married at his estate in Sicily! Isn't it romantic?'

'I suppose,' said Jonathan.

'Anyway, pater was invited to attend the wedding and he told us not to expect him back before the Nones. Yes, Lupus?'

Lupus had been writing on his wax tablet. Now he held it up:

FORUM OF THE CORPORATIONS?

'What about the Forum of the Corporations?'

Lupus used his two hands to mime a fluttering butterfly, then shaded his eyes, as if searching for someone.

'Good idea!' said Flavia. 'You try to find man with the butterfly birthmark at the Forum of the Corporations. I'll go with Jonathan to the main forum. When the gongs clang midday, men will start coming out of the law-courts on their way to the baths. I'm sure one of us will be able to find that witness.'

It took Lupus no time at all to find out the name of the mysterious witness.

Remembering Miriam's description of the man, he etched a simple portrait on his wax tablet. First he drew a face with a long nose and high forehead. Then he added a small butterfly shape over the left eyebrow. Finally, as the gongs clanged noon, he waited for the stream of men to emerge from the Forum of the Corporations on their way to their preferred bath-houses. As they began to pour out of the main exit, he held up the wax tablet in his right hand and pointed at it with his left.

A few curious men gathered round the portrait, attracting others who wanted to see what they were looking at. Soon there was a lively crowd, with some men jostling to see.

'IT'S PAPILLIO, THE DECURION!' boomed a tall, thin man. Praeco – one of Ostia's town criers – was incapable of speaking in a normal voice.

'Papillio?' said another . 'Are you sure?'

'OF COURSE I'M SURE,' thundered Praeco. 'SEE THE BUTTERFLY-SHAPED BIRTHMARK OVER HIS EYEBROW?'

'No, it's Didius,' offered someone else. 'That's not a birthmark, it's just a smudge.'

'It's not a smudge,' said a freedman in his soft conical cap. 'You meant to draw that, didn't you, boy?'

Lupus nodded.

'What's the matter, boy?' said a man with a squint. 'Ox tread on your tongue?'

'Shut up, you fool!' hissed a bald Ethiopian. 'That's the boy what's had his tongue cut out. You be careful how you talk to him. He's a ship owner, he is. Might employ you and your sorry crew one day.'

'Oh. Sorry, boy,' said Squint. 'I meant no disrespect.'

Lupus shrugged, then pointed urgently at the drawing and raised his eyebrows expectantly.

'IF THE BOY MEANT TO DRAW THE BIRTHMARK,' blared the town crier, 'THEN IT'S DEFINITELY PAPILLIO!'

'He means Gnaeus Helvius Papillio, the decurion,' explained Conical Cap. 'You know: member of the city council.'

Lupus nodded enthusiastically and wrote the name on the other leaf of his wax tablet.

'Papillio has a bigger chin,' offered someone.

Lupus quickly rubbed out the chin he had drawn and replaced it with a bigger chin, then held up the tablet again.

'THINNER EYEBROWS!' boomed Praeco.

'Bigger ears!' came the light voice of a eunuch.

'And some frown lines on his forehead,' added Conical Cap.

Lupus used his thumb to smooth the wax and the tip of his bronze stylus to make the necessary adjustments.

Finally they all agreed. The portrait on Lupus's tablet showed the decurion Gnaeus Helvius Papillio, a bachelor who lived on the fourth floor of the Garden Apartments down by the Marina Gate.

'Miriam! Uncle Gaius! Where are you?' called Flavia, as she and her friends followed the dogs up the gravel path of her uncle's Laurentum Lodge. It had taken them over an hour to walk there, but it was a glorious afternoon.

To their right, the silvery-green leaves of three olive trees gleamed. A dozen brown hens had been pecking contentedly at the gravel path, but as Scuto ran to greet them they scattered among the vine rows.

'Scuto! Stop chasing the chickens!' Flavia scolded. 'Why can't you be good, like Nipur and Tigris?' Scuto gazed up at her, panting happily and wagged his tail. Flavia gave him a quick pat and called out again, 'Uncle Gaius?'

The front door squeaked open and an old slave appeared between the two wooden columns of the small porch. He smiled broadly, revealing a single tooth.

'Hello, Senex,' cried Flavia. 'Is Uncle Gaius in?'

'Gone to Rome with Dromo,' replied Senex in a quavering voice. Flavia nodded and smiled. Dromo was the other slave at the Laurentum Lodge. He was not quite as ancient as Senex, having four teeth instead of just one. She knew her uncle and Miriam could not afford proper slaves and had taken the two old men in out of kindness.

'The master and Dromo should be back soon,' quavered Senex. 'The mistress is in her bedroom.' He shuffled to one side so that Flavia and her three friends could enter. The dogs stayed outside to investigate interesting smells.

'Miriam!' called Flavia. She led the way through the little garden courtyard and eagerly flung back the curtain to Miriam's bedroom.

'Oh, I'm sorry!' said Flavia. 'I didn't know you had a visitor.'

Miriam was sitting on her bed combing a doll's hair.

A lovely girl of fourteen or fifteen sat beside her. As Flavia and her friends filled the doorway, the girl jumped up and regarded them with large brown eyes. She had pale skin and a mass of wavy hair the colour of dark copper. It was pulled back from her smooth forehead and contained by a hairnet.

'Hello, Jonathan, Flavia, Nubia and Lupus!' Miriam put down the doll and tried to rise. But her swollen belly impeded her and she fell back onto the bed, giggling. The auburn-haired girl smiled and helped Miriam to her feet.

Miriam turned to them and said breathlessly, 'This is my dear friend Hephzibah; the one I was telling you about. Hephzibah, that's my little brother Jonathan. And Flavia, and Nubia, and that's Lupus.'

'Oh!' cried Hephzibah, and clapped her hands in delight. 'It's baby Jonathan!'

Lupus raised his eyebrows and Jonathan said, 'What?'

Hephzibah turned and looked at Jonathan's sister. 'Miriam, do you remember the day we stole baby Jonathan from his basket and pretended to be mothers?'

'Yes!' Miriam laughed. 'We unwrapped his swaddling clothes to see what he looked like.'

'So tiny and perfect.'

Lupus guffawed and Jonathan scowled. 'I wasn't *that* tiny,' he muttered.

'Oh, Hephzibah!' Miriam gave a strange sobbing laugh. She caught her friend's hands and for a brief moment they exchanged an intense look, which Flavia could not decipher.

Still holding Hephzibah's hands, Miriam turned to the four friends. 'Please tell us you have good news,' she said. 'Tell us you've found the man who witnessed Hephzibah's manumission?'

Flavia nodded and patted Lupus on the back.

'Yes,' she said, 'we have good news.'

SCROLL III

Half an hour later they were all sitting in a small rose garden behind the Laurentum Lodge, drinking lemon barley water and eating dried mulberries, when the wooden gate squeaked open and old Senex appeared.

'Pliny is here,' he quavered. 'Brought him like you asked.'

'Thank you, Senex,' said Miriam, rising to her feet. She went to greet the young man coming through the open gateway into the garden.

'Dear Gaius,' she said. 'Welcome.' She turned to Senex. 'Let me know as soon as my husband returns.' The old slave tugged his wispy grey forelock and nodded, and the garden gate squeaked shut behind him.

Gaius Plinius Secundus looked just as Flavia remembered him. He was about eighteen, of medium height, with a mop of brown hair, rumpled eyebrows and keen black eyes.

Without taking his eyes from Miriam's face, he bent to pat the dogs. Flavia and Nubia exchanged a knowing glance. It was obvious he was still infatuated with her.

'You remember my brother Jonathan, don't you?' said Miriam, flushing under his adoring gaze. 'And Flavia, Nubia and Lupus?'

Pliny stood upright and reluctantly looked at the others.

'Hello,' he said. 'It's good to see you again. How have you all been this past year?'

For a brief moment Flavia considered telling him that they had fought beasts in the new amphitheatre, rescued kidnapped children from the Greek island of Rhodes, pursued a fugitive across half the Greek mainland and raced chariots in the Circus Maximus. Instead she replied: 'Busy. We've been busy.'

'I also,' said Pliny. 'I've been studying rhetoric up in Rome. I've just come back to prepare for the Saturnalia. Your sister and her friend were lucky to find me at home yesterday.' Here he turned his attention back to Miriam, who had resumed her seat.

'Do please sit down, Gaius,' she said, and patted the empty chair between her and Hephzibah. 'Will you have some lemon barley water? Or do you prefer hot spiced wine?'

'Barley water is fine.' He sat on the wooden chair.

'Lupus found the witness,' said Miriam, pouring Pliny's drink.

'Witness?' Pliny gazed adoringly at Miriam.

'The man who witnessed Hephzibah's manumission.' Miriam set the beaker before Pliny. 'You said you needed him to appear when you take Hephzibah to see the magistrate.'

'Oh! Yes. The witness.' Pliny reached into his shoulder bag, pulled out a wax tablet and turned to Hephzibah. 'What's his name?'

'Gnaeus Helvius Papillio,' said Hephzibah in her pleasantly accented voice. 'He looks like this.' She pushed Lupus's open wax tablet across the table.

'Of course!' said Pliny. 'I know this man. I'm sorry, Miriam. I should have guessed from what you told me. Papillio's name means "butterfly". I let you down badly.'

'No, Gaius, you didn't let us down. But what do we do now?'

Pliny drained his beaker, plunked it down emphatically and stood up.

'Nothing. You do nothing. I will issue Papillio with a summons requiring him to come to court. Not tomorrow – it's nefas – but the day after, the day before the Nones. Will I see you there?'

'Yes,' said Miriam. 'I'll be there.' She squeezed Hephzibah's hand. 'I want to support my dear friend.'

'We'll be there, too,' said Flavia, 'if Aristo agrees to make it part of our lessons. After all,' she added, 'we found the witness.'

'Excellent,' said Pliny, his eyes never leaving Miriam's face. 'Then I will see you the day after tomorrow. Good-bye, Hephzibah. Good-bye, Miriam.' He managed to tear his gaze away from her for a moment and smile down at the rest of them. 'Good-bye, my young friends!'

At the garden gate he turned and added. 'By the way, the hearing won't be in the basilica, but rather in the forum. Probably by the little shrine of Ceres. After all,' he added. 'It's only a formality.'

Two days later, early on the day before the Nones, they all walked to the forum to watch Papillio testify that Hephzibah was free.

'Aristo,' said Flavia. 'How do you set a slave free?'

Aristo was the handsome young Corinthian who had

been her tutor for three years. He had tanned skin, hair the colour of bronze and intelligent brown eyes.

'One method,' he began, 'is for the master or mistress to invite the slave to recline beside them, in the presence of witnesses.'

'That's how I freed Nubia,' said Flavia, catching her friend's hand and giving it a quick squeeze. 'What else?'

'The official method is to free them in the presence of an official: a consul or praetor, if you want to go right to the top. But a duovir or an aedile will do today. Even a decurion.'

'Who are those people?' A pretty frown creased Nubia's forehead.

Aristo raised both eyebrows. 'Can anyone tell Nubia the difference between a duovir, aedile and decurion?'

'A duovir,' said Jonathan, 'is one of two men who run Ostia, like the two consuls in Rome. The aediles look after public buildings, especially temples and baths. The decurions are members of the town council. They're more common,' he added. 'I think there are a hundred of them here in Ostia.'

'Correct.' Aristo flashed Jonathan an approving smile.

'Are there other ways to make slaves free?' asked Nubia.

'Yes,' said Aristo. 'The other most common method of manumission is for a master to set free some of his slaves in his will. That way they serve him as long as he lives, then form a grateful crowd of freedmen at his funeral. In that case, the seven witnesses of the will act as witnesses to the manumission,' he added.

'Like Dives,' said Jonathan. 'He freed about a dozen of his slaves. They were all there celebrating.'

'Don't you mean mourning?' said Flavia.

'A bit of both, I suppose,' said Jonathan, as they passed the theatre. 'I wouldn't want people celebrating at my funeral. I'd want them all to be miserable.'

'We promise we'll be miserable,' said Flavia, and Lupus chuckled.

'Don't laugh,' muttered Jonathan. 'You might regret it.'

'What do you mean?'

'I keep having a dream.'

'Bad dream?' asked Nubia.

Jonathan nodded. 'The same one, every single night.'

'Like Nubia's nightmares a few months ago?' said Flavia.

'Yes, but it's not like an ordinary dream. It's so real. It's more like the dream I had before Vesuvius erupted.'

Lupus gave Jonathan a look of alarm and Nubia asked, 'What is in your bad dream?'

'I dream I'm watching a funeral procession on a foggy day—' Jonathan took a deep breath '— and I think it's mine.'

'Jonathan!' cried Flavia as they all made the sign against evil. 'Don't say such a thing!'

'Poor Jonathan,' said Nubia, and she patted his back.

'Well,' said Aristo, 'it's my job to keep you safe. I'll try as hard as I can to make sure nothing happens to any of you.'

Flavia made the sign against evil one more time, just for good measure, as they emerged into the open space of the forum.

It was a cloudy morning and smoke from the dawn sacrifices still hung in the cold air.

'Behold!' cried Nubia. 'Pliny. And Phrixus, too!'

'Where?' said Aristo, looking around.

'There! Between small round fountain and Temple of Rome and Augustus.'

'Oh, I see them!' said Flavia. 'By the shrine to Ceres. And look! There's Miriam and Hephzibah and Dromo. That angry-looking fat man must be the magistrate.'

'And there's the town crier,' said Jonathan.

'GNAEUS HELVIUS PAPILLIO,' bellowed Praeco from his plinth, 'DECURION OF OSTIA, RESIDENT OF THE GARDEN APARTMENTS. COME TO THE FORUM TO CONFIRM A MANUMISSION!'

'By Hercules!' breathed Aristo, as they drew closer to the circular shrine of Ceres, 'She's so pregnant!'

Miriam came to meet them, a worried expression on her lovely face. 'Jonathan! Flavia!' she cried. 'He's not here yet! Papillio isn't here.'

'I can't understand it,' said Pliny, coming up behind her. 'I sent notification yesterday. It's just lucky Nonius needed to use the latrines,' he added. 'He's not back to complain . . . yet.'

'Oh Flavia!' cried Miriam. 'What will we do? The magistrate says we have to produce the witness today or Hephzibah will forfeit the case.'

'GNAEUS HELVIUS PAPILLIO,' blasted Praeco behind them, 'IF YOU DO NOT APPEAR, THE PLAINTIFF WILL FORFEIT HER CASE!'

The magistrate – a fat, sour-faced man in a red-bordered toga – glared up at the town crier and said something to his clerk, who made a note on a wax tablet.

'I can't understand it,' repeated Pliny. 'I sent Papillio the summons yesterday. Phrixus delivered it in person, didn't you?'

'I did,' said Phrixus. He turned to Flavia and said: 'It is good to see you again.'

'It's good to see you, too, Phrixus,' said Flavia.

Phrixus turned back to Pliny. 'Shall I go and look for Papillio in the basilica?' he asked. 'Maybe he went there by mistake.'

'Good idea,' said Pliny. 'Do that.'

Phrixus hurried off towards the basilica.

A swarthy young man ran up; he was breathing heavily. 'So,' he said, 'where is your so-called-witness? Is he still not here?'

'That's Nonius Celer,' said Jonathan in Flavia's ear.

She nodded and studied Dives' heir. He was a tall, good-looking man with dark, woolly hair, light brown skin and green eyes. He wore a dark grey cloak over a rust-red tunic.

'I'm a busy man,' said Nonius, 'and I have an estate to run. I've been waiting nearly half an hour for this Papillio.'

'Shall we look for him, too?' said Flavia to Pliny. 'We know where he lives: on the fourth floor of the Garden Apartments by the Marina Gate. We'll—'

'GNAEUS HELVIUS PAPILLIO,' thundered Praeco, 'DECURION OF OSTIA AND RESIDENT OF THE GARDEN APARTMENTS YOU ARE SUMMONED TO THE FORUM TO CONFIRM A MANUMISSION!'

'We'll go right now,' continued Flavia.

'You'd better,' growled the magistrate. 'If you fail to produce the witness in the next half hour, then not only will this young woman lose her case, but she'll have to pay a fine for wasting my valuable time.'

★

A few minutes later, Nubia and her friends stood before a tall red-brick apartment building.

Nubia did not understand how people could bear to live in such lofty buildings. Jonathan told stories of tall apartment blocks collapsing without notice, but Flavia said that only happened in Rome.

Nubia's head tipped back as she looked up all five storeys. Instead of a red-tiled roof she saw green foliage peeping above the upper level. 'Behold. There are trees on the roof,' she said.

'It must have a roof-garden,' said Flavia, and looked at Lupus. 'Is this it?'

Lupus nodded and held up his wax tablet. Nubia saw what he had written:

GARDEN APARTMENTS BY MARINA GATE
FOURTH FLOOR

'It's big,' said Flavia, 'but luckily there are four of us. I'll take the eastern side, Jonathan you take west, Nubia south and Lupus north. Start at one end of the corridor and work your way along. Just knock at doors. Or ask anyone you see. Someone must know where Papillio lives.'

Nubia nodded and followed her ex-mistress. They passed through a dim, vaulted entry way and emerged into a bright, spacious courtyard with a large rainwater pool at its centre. Nubia saw cooking hearths at the north end of the courtyard and latrines at the south. There were no trees in this courtyard, but a few shrubs had been planted near the latrines, and a pretty herb-bed surrounded the pool. The outside of the large building had been blank and uninviting, with small windows in a flat expanse of the brick; inside, she could see that each of the apartments had larger windows overlooking the balcony corridors and courtyard beyond.

Flavia indicated the stairs at the southwest corner and Nubia dutifully began to go up them. They were made of gleaming white marble. The thought occurred to her that this would make them easier to climb at night. She went up four flights, then turned to approach the door nearest the stairs. She was surprised to find it slightly ajar. As she tentatively knocked, it swung open.

Almost at her feet lay the man with the butterfly birthmark: flat on his back, his eyes open but unseeing. A glistening smear of blood on the white marble floor showed how he had crawled across the room and almost made it to the door before he died.

SCROLL IV

Nubia stared in horror at the dead man lying at her feet. Blood had soaked his cream tunic and turned it dark red.

Suddenly his staring eyes moved to lock with hers.

Nubia screamed: he was still alive.

She was about to turn and run, but then she saw the terror in his eyes and a thought entered her mind: comfort him. He is dying.

'Papillio?' she whispered.

He groaned, and reached up a bloody hand imploringly. She knelt beside him and took his out-stretched hand.

He opened his mouth, but no words emerged.

From the balcony corridor behind her came the sound of running footsteps.

'Don't worry, Gnaeus,' she said, somehow remembering his praenomen. 'People are coming to help.' She attempted a smile. 'Do not try to speak.'

He opened his mouth again, and managed to gasp: 'I didn't tell . . . Quick!' She nodded as if she understood, and he seemed to take courage from this. Even as the light in his eyes faded, he managed to say: 'Find the other six . . . By Hercules!' Then she heard the death rattle and she knew he was gone.

Outside the footsteps skidded to a halt. Nubia turned to see Flavia and Lupus arriving together in the open doorway. A moment later, Jonathan, Pliny, Phrixus and the swarthy man called Nonius appeared in the balcony corridor behind them.

For a moment they all stared in horror at the dead man.

Then Nonius fainted, and Flavia began to scream.

'Are you certain?' said Flavia to Nubia an hour later. 'Are you certain that's what he said?'

'Yes,' said Nubia, taking a sip of mint tea. 'His last words were: *I didn't tell. Quick. Find the other six. By Hercules.*'

Nubia lay wrapped in a blanket on the divan back at Jonathan's house. Jonathan's father, Doctor Mordecai, had bled her to ease the shock. Then, after commanding her to rest, he had hurried to the scene of the murder in order to examine the corpse.

'Nubia, are you sure Papillio didn't say anything else?' said Flavia. 'That doesn't make sense.'

'Master of the Universe, Flavia!' muttered Jonathan. 'Leave Nubia alone. She's just had a terrible shock. A man died in her arms. And she's just had a cup of her own blood drained from her.'

'He's right,' said Aristo. 'Nubia's had an awful shock. Thank the gods Miriam didn't see the body. I hope she and her friend got back to Laurentum all right.'

'I'm sorry, Nubia,' said Flavia, 'but that poor man was murdered. And we've got to find out why.'

Nubia nodded.

Lupus held up his wax tablet. He had written one word: SUICIDE?

'I don't think so, Lupus,' said Flavia. 'Why would he fall on his sword and then try to crawl for help?'

'Also,' said Jonathan, 'his last words were: *I didn't tell.* As if someone had threatened to make him talk and he refused and then they stabbed him.'

Lupus pursed his lips and nodded, as if to say: Good point.

Suddenly there was a thunderous pounding on the front door and Tigris started to bark.

Flavia glanced at Jonathan. 'That doesn't sound like your father,' she said.

'No,' agreed Jonathan.

A moment later Delilah appeared in the wide doorway of the tablinum.

'It was soldiers,' she said breathlessly. 'They wanted Nubia. I say you are next door because they want to arrest you.'

'Why would they want to arrest Nubia?' said Flavia with a frown.

'Maybe they think she murdered Papillio,' said Jonathan.

'What?' cried Flavia.

'Delilah,' said Jonathan, 'what were their exact words?'

The letters on the slave-girl's forehead crinkled as she frowned. 'That they want to arrest and interrogate Nubia. They say she must come because she is a slave.'

Flavia frowned. 'But Nubia's not a slave. I freed her in Surrentum over a year ago.'

'In the presence of a magistrate?' asked Aristo.

Next door they could hear Scuto and Nipur barking, as the soldiers pounded on Flavia's door.

'No,' said Flavia. 'I freed Nubia in the presence of

Publius Pollius Felix and his family. I told you this morning. I invited her to recline on the couch beside me.'

Aristo stood up and his face grew pale. 'Flavia,' he said, 'did you ever pay the slave-tax?'

'What's that?'

'Dear gods,' said Aristo. 'You didn't do it properly. She's not free. Nubia's officially still a slave.'

Flavia stared blankly at him. 'But you said that if you invite a slave to recline with you, then they're free.'

'Yes, but you have to register their manumission in your home town, and then you have to pay twenty per cent of the purchase price.'

Flavia shrugged. 'I can do that.'

'You don't understand. Roman law says that slaves who witness a crime can not give evidence unless they've been tortured. A Roman citizen just died in Nubia's arms. If they want her to give evidence, and if she's still technically a slave, that means they *have* to torture her. It's the law. There's no time to officially free her now.'

The pounding came again at the door, so loud that the whole house seemed to shake.

'They're back!' cried Delilah. 'Someone must have told them Nubia is here.'

'Run, Nubia!' said Flavia, pulling her dazed friend off the divan. 'Go out the back door!'

Nubia's blanket slipped to the floor and she stood trembling, her left elbow still bandaged where Doctor Mordecai had made the cut in order to bleed her.

'Where?' she whispered. 'Where can I go?'

'I don't know,' cried Flavia hysterically. As the front door splintered and crashed open, she shoved Nubia towards the back of the house. 'Just run! Run, Nubia. Run!'

Nubia ran.

She ran through Jonathan's inner garden and out the back door and straight into the necropolis, the city of the dead. The low dark clouds hung menacingly above her.

She ran among the umbrella pines, weaving back and forth, not daring to look behind to see if they were pursuing her. The blood sang in her ears while her running feet beat a terrified rhythm.

Nubia ran.

She could smell the rain and feel the charged air.

She had to find shelter. She could go to the Geminus family tomb, but if they searched the necropolis that would be the first place they would look. She must go to another tomb. One which Flavia and her friends knew about, but no one else.

A drop of rain spattered onto her cheek. Then another. And another. From her left came a flash and the crack of thunder.

Nubia veered right, weaving between the tall umbrella pines.

Above her the heavens opened and the rain poured down.

Nubia ran.

'Master of the Universe,' said Mordecai, coming into the tablinum. 'What happened to our front door?' He was shaking out his dripping cloak.

Flavia lifted her face from her hands and looked at him. 'Oh, Doctor Mordecai!' she cried. 'It's Nubia!'

A flash of lightning illuminated his concerned face and a moment later came a huge crash of thunder.

'What?' cried Mordecai. 'What's happened to Nubia?'

'Soldiers came to arrest her,' said Aristo, 'claiming that she's still a slave.'

'Dear Lord,' said Mordecai, his face pale. 'That means . . .'

'We know what it means,' said Jonathan. 'We're going to try to find her, as soon as it stops raining.'

'I should have gone with her,' sobbed Flavia. 'Or sent Nipur with her. But I just pushed her out of the door. She doesn't even have her lionskin cloak.'

Lupus awkwardly patted her arm and Jonathan said, 'Don't cry, Flavia. They took us by surprise. We all panicked.'

'What's happening to us?' said Flavia through her tears. 'Why did they kill that poor butterfly man? And who told the officials that Nubia might not have been properly freed?'

'I think,' said Aristo slowly, 'that whoever committed the murder wants to frighten you off. That's why they've gone after Nubia.'

'What did you discover, father?' asked Jonathan. 'Did you see the body?'

'Yes. I saw the body.' Another flash of lightning came, further off.

'Could it have been suicide?'

'I doubt it.' Mordecai sat on the striped divan and looked around at their concerned faces. 'Papillio was killed by a single blow from a gladius – the short thrusting sword of a legionary. We found it in his apartment, lying on the floor at the other end of the trail of blood. There were brackets for it on the wall.

34

Papillio obviously kept it there as a trophy.' Mordecai looked around at them with his heavy-lidded dark eyes. 'Not long before Nubia found him, someone came to see him. They talked and I presume they argued. The killer probably took the sword from the wall, stabbed Papillio once, then dropped the weapon and ran. But it was a clumsy blow. Or perhaps a hasty one. Instead of killing him instantly . . . I reckon it took him nearly half an hour to die.'

'Oh!' cried Flavia. 'The poor man!'

From the northwest came a low growl of thunder. In the garden, the shrubs trembled under the beating rain.

Mordecai accepted a beaker of steaming mint tea from Delilah and sipped it thoughtfully. 'I'm afraid there is something much more sinister here than the case of a Jewish slave-girl being set free.'

Another crash of thunder seemed to emphasise his statement.

Flavia took out a handkerchief and blew her nose. 'You're right, Doctor Mordecai,' she said. 'We've got to find out more about Hephzibah. She's the key.'

Lupus nodded and pointed at Flavia, as if to say: She's right.

Mordecai shook his head. 'No,' he said. 'That's not what I'm saying. I'm saying you should leave this case alone.'

'I agree with Doctor Mordecai,' said Aristo, and added gently. 'I know you think of yourself as a truth-seeker, Flavia, but this is an ugly case. A man has been murdered. Let it go.'

'I can't let it go. We're all involved. Miriam, too.' Here Flavia looked pointedly at Aristo. 'Whoever did it must be stopped. We owe it to Miriam, and to her friend Hephzibah, and to the murdered man. And to poor Nubia. We must solve this mystery,' she said fiercely. 'Or at least try.'

'Very well,' said Mordecai at last. 'But only with our help and close supervision. Agreed?' He looked at Aristo.

Aristo gave a nod. 'Our *close* supervision,' he said.

'Thank you, Aristo. Thank you, Doctor Mordecai.' Flavia wiped her wet cheeks with the back of her hand. 'Now, where shall we start?'

'Why don't we find out more about the key to this case,' suggested Jonathan.

'Hephzibah?' said Flavia.

Jonathan nodded. 'Hephzibah.'

It was still raining hard, so they hired a covered carruca for the drive to Laurentum.

It had been decided that Aristo would stay at Jonathan's house to help Caudex repair the front door and that Mordecai would go with them to the Laurentum Lodge. As they left the Laurentum Gate and headed for the coastal road, Flavia sat in the back of the carruca, looking out and calling Nubia's name over and over. There was no reply from the dripping woods and Flavia's voice was hoarse by the time they reached the Lodge.

Miriam waved from the porch as the carruca crunched up the gravel drive. She came carefully down the rain-slicked steps holding her palla over her head to keep off the rain. Gaius's huge mastiff Ferox followed her to the gate.

'Hephzibah's not here,' she said, when her father explained their mission. 'She's up the road at Pliny's estate. He dropped me here and then drove her straight there. He's offered his protection until this matter is settled.'

'Thank you, my daughter,' said Mordecai. 'We will go straight there.' He twitched the reins to turn the carruca, then clicked the mules into motion.

'Stop and have some lunch with me on your way back,' Miriam called after them. 'Gaius has gone to Rome and he won't be back until later.'

The rain stopped as they pulled up the circular drive of the magnificent Laurentine villa. Pliny himself came to meet them.

'Hephzibah is at Dives' old estate,' he said. 'She went to collect her things just before the rain started. Phrixus took the carruca back to Ostia to do some shopping, and I asked him to drop her off. She said she'd return here on foot, and she should be back by now . . . I've been debating whether or not to send a slave with a mule for her.'

'We'll go,' said Mordecai. 'And we'll bring her back here. Which estate is it?'

'Back the way you came,' said Pliny, pointing north. 'The turning is just past the Lodge. It's not far at all. I'll have the slaves warm some wine for you.'

But they never had warm wine at Pliny's or lunch at the Laurentum Lodge. When they arrived at the coastal estate of Lucius Nonius Celer, they found the opulent villa in turmoil.

'What's happening?' Mordecai called down to a running slave.

'Murder!' said the slave eagerly. 'She's murdered one of his freedmen! I'm just going to tell the field-workers.'

'Who?' Flavia pulled back the canvas flaps of the

carruca so they could all see the slave. 'Who's been murdered?'

'Mercator. They found him in her cubicle with his head bashed in. And the girl crouched over him.'

'Girl?' repeated Flavia. 'Which girl?'

'That Jewish girl who claims she's free. Hephzibah.'

SCROLL V

'Who are you?' cried Nonius, as Mordecai shouldered his way to the front of an excited crowd in the atrium. Nonius had been watching two slaves tie Hephzibah to a column. One of them must have pulled the hairnet from her head because her copper-coloured hair was falling loose around her shoulders.

'I am Mordecai ben Ezra.' The doctor gave a very un-Roman bow. 'Are you Lucius Nonius Celer?'

'I am.' Nonius's left eye was bruised and his chest was rising and falling. In his left hand he held a whipping reed and Flavia saw it was stained brown with old blood. 'What are you doing here?'

'We are friends of that young woman,' said Mordecai. 'Please release her.'

'Are you mad?' Nonius's left hand clenched and unclenched on the handle of the long reed. 'She murdered a man and when I tried to stop her from running away she fought like a harpy. Look what she did to me!' He pointed to his swollen eye.

'No!' sobbed Hephzibah, twisting to look over her shoulder. 'I didn't do that! And I didn't kill that man.'

'Please release her,' repeated Mordecai, quietly but firmly.

'Not until I've whipped the truth out of her,' said

Nonius. He held up a small leather pouch in his right hand. 'Where did you get all this gold?' he snarled at Hephzibah. 'You stole it from Mercator, didn't you?'

'No!' said Hephzibah. 'It's mine! I told you: a friend gave it me, so that I could buy my freedom from you and—'

'Wool fluff!' cried Nonius. 'If you wanted to buy your freedom why didn't you come straight to me?' He nodded at the biggest slave, who tore the back of Hephzibah's tunic from the neck, exposing her naked back.

'It's my gold!' sobbed Hephzibah. 'Jonathan! Your sister gave it to me.'

'Liar!' Nonius raised the rod.

'I will ask you not do that, sir,' said Mordecai, stepping between Nonius and Hephzibah. 'That girl is currently under the protection of Gaius Plinius Secundus, your neighbour and a friend of the Emperor Titus.'

At the mention of Titus's name a change came over Nonius. His breathing slowed. His eyes lost their feverish gleam. Finally he tossed the bloodstained reed onto the floor.

'May I see the gold?' asked Mordecai.

Nonius paused for a moment, then thrust the coin purse angrily into the doctor's open hand.

Mordecai opened the bag and looked in. 'I recognise these coins. They are part of my daughter's dowry. This girl did not steal from the dead man. My daughter gave her these coins.'

'You'll have to prove that,' said Nonius. 'And she's not going back to Pliny's villa. I've summoned the vigiles from Ostia. She'll stay locked up in prison until I bring her to trial and find the truth.'

'We can take her into our custody, if you wish,' said Mordecai calmly.

'I do not wish.' Nonius's swollen eye gave him an unpleasant leer. 'You're a Jew like her, aren't you?'

'I am a Jew and a Roman citizen,' said Mordecai. 'I am also a doctor and I would like to see the body of the murdered man.'

Nonius's good eye narrowed. 'What can you do for Mercator? He's dead.'

'Nonetheless, I would like to see the body.' Doctor Mordecai countered Nonius's menacing stare with a heavy-lidded gaze.

For a long moment the two men looked at each other, then Nonius shrugged. 'As you wish. He's still lying in her cubicle.' He turned to a slave. 'Elpias. Show them the body.'

'Thank you,' said Mordecai. He turned to follow the slave and then turned back. 'Please, Nonius Celer, will you untie that girl and cover her until the vigiles arrive?'

Hephzibah's sleeping cubicle at the back of the villa was so small that Doctor Mordecai had to crouch to enter it. One glimpse at the dead body on the floor convinced Flavia to stay outside with Jonathan. She was happy to let Lupus follow the doctor in.

Mordecai muttered an oath as his head struck the low-vaulted roof of the cell. 'Master of the Universe! I can't even stand upright in here.' He knelt over the corpse. 'Killed by a single blow to the right temple,' he murmured presently. 'Death seems to have been instantaneous. But where is the weapon?'

Lupus gave a grunt and Flavia saw his hand appear, framed in the doorway and holding a ceramic jug.

'Ah,' said Mordecai, taking the jug by the handle and examining it. 'This is certainly heavy enough. But there is no trace of blood or hair on it. And there is still water in the bottom. Where did you get this?'

Lupus pointed to the back of the small cubicle. Flavia and Jonathan cracked skulls as they both put their heads in the small doorway to get a better look.

'Ow!' said Flavia, and rubbed her head. Suddenly she stopped rubbing and looked at Mordecai. 'If the jug was used as a weapon,' she said, 'wouldn't the water have spilled onto the floor? Or onto his clothes?' She allowed herself another quick peek at the body. The dead man's eyes gazed up at the low-vaulted ceiling with an expression of mild surprise. Then she saw the bloody dent above his right eyebrow and she hastily looked away.

'Yes,' said Mordecai. 'If that jug was the murder weapon, then I should expect to find water here. But apart from a little blood – a very little blood for such a head-wound – this earthen floor is completely dry. Also,' he looked around, 'I don't see how a person could strike a death blow in such a confined space. There's barely room for a man and a boy in here.'

'Maybe he wasn't killed in here,' said Jonathan.

Lupus grunted his agreement.

'And maybe Hephzibah didn't do it!' cried Flavia.

Mordecai gave her a keen look. Then he turned his head to look over his shoulder, 'Lupus,' he said, 'while we interview Hephzibah, I want you to do what you do so well.'

Lupus raised his eyebrows questioningly.

'I want you to look around the villa for signs of a

spillage. Or of a spillage which has been cleaned. But be careful: don't let anyone see you.'

Lupus nodded, his eyes shining.

Flavia frowned. 'Spillage?' she said. 'What kind of spillage?' Then her eyes widened and she answered her own question. 'Oh,' she breathed, 'blood!'

The atrium was almost empty when they returned; Jonathan saw that Nonius and most of his household had gone. There were only two sullen slaves flanking the exit. And the woman he had seen at Dives's funeral was lurking in the shadows behind a column. As soon as the woman saw them she moved quickly towards Jonathan. He remembered her name was Restituta.

'I saw you and your friends arrive,' she said and gripped his arm hard. 'Since I saw you at the funeral there's a rumour been going around among the slaves. I thought you should know.' Restituta brought her mouth close to his ear and said in a barely audible voice. 'They say Dives was murdered. Smothered while he slept.'

Then she released her grip on his arm and hurried out of the atrium.

Jonathan frowned after her, then turned to Hephzibah. She was sitting on a stool in the shelter of the peristyle, her auburn hair tangled and her dark eyes staring blankly ahead. Someone had draped a grey palla round her shoulders to hide her torn tunic. Someone else – or perhaps the same person – had tied one end of a rope around her ankles and the other to a pillar.

'The vigiles obviously haven't arrived yet,' murmured Mordecai. 'That gives us a little time.'

He took a chair from the tablinum and pulled it up

before Hephzibah. Then he sat facing her and began to speak in Aramaic.

Hephzibah replied in the same language, and Jonathan interpreted for Flavia.

'She told Pliny she was going to pick up her things,' said Jonathan after a moment. 'When she reached her sleeping-cubicle she saw Mercator lying on the ground.'

'Did she know him?' said Flavia. 'Ask her if she knew Mercator.'

Hephzibah turned and looked at Flavia. 'I will speak Latin,' she said, and then turned back to Mordecai. 'I only knew Mercator by sight. He was one of my master's freedmen.'

'So he was already dead when you got there?' said Mordecai. He was also speaking Latin now.

'Yes. I must have screamed because a moment later there were slaves outside the door and then Nonius appeared and accused me of killing him. But I didn't! I didn't!'

'Did you strike Nonius?' asked Mordecai gently.

'No! I didn't touch him!' She gazed around at them with pleading brown eyes.

'I believe you,' said Mordecai. 'But I must ask you: Why did you not go straight to Nonius and offer him the gold to buy your freedom?'

'I went to see Priscilla first,' said Hephzibah.

'Who's Priscilla?' asked Flavia.

Hephzibah lowered her eyes. 'Just a slave. A friend. She's pregnant, like Miriam.'

'So you didn't go straight to your cubicle,' said Mordecai. 'You went to see your friend first.'

'Yes.'

'Why didn't you tell us that before?' said Flavia.

'I forgot,' said Hephzibah, her eyes still lowered.

'Hephzibah,' said Mordecai, 'did you see anyone else lurking near your cubicle?'

'No. It was less than an hour ago, around noon. All the other slaves were working.'

'Including Priscilla?' said Flavia.

'Yes. She helps the cook. I went to see her in the kitchen. We spoke for a short time. Then I went to the part of the villa were the sleeping-cubicles are. I was going to get my things before I went to Nonius.'

'What things?' asked Flavia.

Hephzibah kept her head down. 'Two tunics and a palla. A doll my mother gave me. Then I saw the body.' She shuddered.

'Hephzibah,' said Mordecai gently. 'Are you the daughter of David ben Tobias, the priest?'

'Yes!' Hephzibah raised her head and Flavia saw her brown eyes were brimming with tears. 'Did you know him?'

'Very well,' said Mordecai. 'He was a good man, and a good friend. I believe you came to our house several times. Our house in Jerusalem by the Beautiful Gate.'

Hephzibah nodded. 'Yes. I was very little, but I still remember the citron tree in your courtyard and the yellow and blue wall tiles.' Tears wet her cheeks. 'Playing with Miriam in your courtyard – those are the happiest memories of my whole life.'

Nubia woke with a start.

She was curled up in a dim, cramped space. It smelled of charred pine-cones and damp earth.

A tomb. She was in a tomb, with the ashes of the dead.

For a moment she could not think how she came to be here. Then she remembered running in the grave-yard, dizzy from being bled and shivering from cold and shock. She must have fallen asleep.

Outside, the rain had stopped. From the look of the pearly winter light it was mid-afternoon.

She put her head tentatively out the small arched opening of the tomb.

The pine branches overhead were still dripping and she could smell the acrid scent of someone burning damp leaves.

She began to crawl out on hands and knees, because Avita's tomb was built for a child. Then she recoiled. A dead shrew lay outside the little doorway of the tomb. Some woodland creature had killed it and chewed off its head.

She carefully scooped a hole for it in the dirt, used a dead leaf to push it into the hole, and patted earth over its tiny corpse. Then she bowed her head and recited a prayer for the dead.

As she stood up she felt an ache in the crook of her left elbow, where doctor Mordecai had cut her skin. There was a spot of blood on the linen bandage, and there was blood on her butter-coloured tunic, too. That blood was not hers; it belonged to poor Papillio.

Suddenly a strong hand griped her wrist.

Nubia screamed.

SCROLL VI

Nubia screamed and kicked and thrashed her arms, but the man had grabbed her from behind and now he was pinning her wrists to her side with one strong arm while he covered her screaming mouth with his free hand.

'Nubia!' A familiar voice and warm breath in her ear. 'Nubia, it's me, Aristo.'

Her knees gave way with relief and she almost collapsed. But he caught her and turned her and now he was hugging her tightly. Her nose was buried in the soft linen of his fawn tunic and she could smell his scent and feel his heart pounding against her cheek.

She wrapped her arms around his slim, muscular waist and tried to keep the tears in.

Aristo had found her! He loved her. He loved her as she loved him.

She held him tighter, wishing he would never let her go, but presently he did, kissing the top of her head before he held her at arm's length.

'Look at you!' he laughed. 'What a state! Mud on your cheek, dirt under your fingernails, blood on your tunic. We need to get you to the baths.'

She nodded, too happy for words.

'I know where to take you,' he said. 'The perfect

place. You'll be safe there. They have a little hot plunge and a big guard dog.' His voice was husky with emotion. 'She can look after you and you can look after her.'

All the blood seemed to drain to Nubia's feet. She gazed up into his warm brown eyes, so animated by love, and she felt a terrible chill.

'Where?' she whispered, hardly able to trust her voice.

'To Miriam, of course. Come. I have a horse tethered just over there. We can be at the Laurentum Lodge in a quarter of an hour.'

'There she is!' said Lucius Nonius Celer to the vigiles. 'There's the murderess!' He led two armed men into the atrium and gestured at Hephzibah, still tethered to a column. 'Take her to Ostia and throw her in the cells!'

'Are you calling her to trial?' said one of the soldiers to Nonius. 'Because we have no authority to hold her until someone brings a suit.'

'Of course I'm bringing a suit!' Anger darkened Nonius' already swarthy face. 'She killed my former patron's freedman, Mercator. And I now have reason to suspect that she may also have killed Dives himself.'

'What?' cried Flavia.

'No!' cried Hephzibah. 'My master was kind to me. I would never hurt him.'

'By Hercules!' Nonius's good eye opened wide. 'I believe you killed that poor magistrate, too! Papillio. You went to his apartments and stabbed him before you met us at the forum.'

'That makes no sense,' said Mordecai. 'Why would this girl want to kill the one person who could prove she was free?' His voice was calm but Flavia noticed that his accent was more pronounced, a sure sign that he was upset.

'Perhaps because he was the one person who could prove she *wasn't* free!' said Nonius. 'I'm going to hire the best lawyers money can buy. And I promise you: I will find the truth!'

Aristo untethered a broad-backed bay gelding named Fortis that Nubia recognised from the Laurentum Gate stables. Flavia's father often chose this horse when he wanted to ride out to see his brother.

There was no mounting block nearby, so Aristo led the gelding to a small marble grave marker and, muttering an apology to the spirits of the dead, he stepped onto it and then up onto the horse.

He leant down and when Nubia grasped his extended forearm, he swung her up behind him.

The saddle was not meant for two and she had to press herself very close to him.

'Hold on,' he said over his shoulder. 'Hold on tight.'

Nubia nodded and wrapped her arms miserably around him. For almost an entire year she had secretly loved him. Today, for one perfect moment, it had seemed that he returned her feelings. But now she knew that the love in his eyes and the beating of his heart was not for her, but for Miriam.

Aristo clicked his tongue and she felt his heels touch the horse's side. Soon they emerged from the pine woods and trotted out onto the Laurentum Road.

The sea appeared on the right, deep cobalt blue with a thousand white horses marching in from the northwest. The wind was sweeping low clouds in from the same direction, so that sometimes she was in brilliant sunshine and others in shadow.

She took a deep breath. The storm-scoured air was fresh and cool, as intoxicating as watered wine. Birds sang in the umbrella pines and sunlit drops of water fell like diamonds onto the sandy road, which was perfect for riders on horseback.

Nubia loved horses almost as much as she loved Aristo. She should have been blissfully happy riding with him on this sparkling afternoon.

But Aristo did not love her, and never would. She suddenly realised that she was a slave after all, and a fugitive slave at that. And there was blood on her tunic from a murdered man.

She turned her head in the direction of the sea, rested her cheek on his back and let the tears flow.

Abruptly she felt his whole body stiffen as he reined in the gelding.

'Pollux!' he cursed. 'Someone's coming. We can't risk them seeing us.'

He kicked the horse's flank and they veered off the road and down into the woods. When they were screened by the thick trunks of the umbrella pines, Aristo expertly turned the horse so they could peer through the branches at the road up ahead.

Nubia could hear it now: the sound of horses' hooves and the jingle of armour and the squeaking wheel of a cart.

Presently a carruca appeared around a bend, travelling in the direction of Ostia, with two riders flanking it.

'By Apollo!' muttered Aristo. 'It is the vigiles!'

'How did they find us?' asked Nubia. She was trembling so much that her teeth were chattering.

'I don't think those particular vigiles are looking for you. I think they're escorting that carriage. There are three people inside; can you see who they are?'

'I can not see inside yet, only that Doctor Mordecai is driving. Maybe the men torture him and force him to reveal where I am hiding.'

'No. Mordecai seems fine.'

'Now I see! It is Flavia and Jonathan inside—'

'And a girl with tangled red hair. She's wearing leather manacles. They're arresting her.'

'That is Hephzibah,' said Nubia. 'We saw her this morning in the forum. Do you not remember? She is Miriam's friend. The one who wants to be free.'

Ostia's basilica was a tall, marble-veneered building at the south-western corner of the forum next to a large temple of Venus. The law court occupied its spacious ground floor, with a gallery giving way to offices on the first floor. At the back of the basilica were four small prison cells where prisoners could be held until they stood trial.

'It wasn't too bad,' said Mordecai as he came down the basilica steps to where Flavia and Jonathan were waiting. 'I convinced them to put her in a cell by herself. Let's hope it stays that way.'

'You mean they could put her in with male criminals?' gasped Flavia.

He nodded grimly, 'If it gets busy. It's the same cell I was privileged to occupy last year,' he added.

'Does she have to stay there?' asked Flavia.

Mordecai nodded. 'Until we've raised the money for her vadimonium.'

'How much?' asked Flavia and Jonathan together.

'Fifty thousand sesterces,' said Mordecai. 'A ridiculous amount for a Jewish slave-girl.'

'We can pay that,' said Jonathan. 'I got all that reward money in September.'

'That's generous of you,' said Mordecai. 'But I'll still need to obtain a promissory note, and the bankers' stalls have closed for today. Hephzibah will have to spend the night here. Not a pleasant prospect.'

'Oh, Doctor Mordecai!' cried Flavia. 'Can't we do something?'

'All we can do,' he said, 'is smuggle her a blanket and some food and perhaps a writing tablet. I have a feeling she's still not telling us everything.'

Miserably, Nubia watched Aristo and Miriam come together.

After the vigiles and the carruca had passed out of sight, Aristo had urged the gelding back up onto the road and galloped all the way to the Laurentum Lodge without slowing. As the foaming horse skidded to a halt at the end of the gravel path, Aristo jumped off, vaulted the gate, ran to the front door and pounded on it. A tearful Miriam opened the front door, and Nubia suspected it was only the sight of her swollen belly that prevented Aristo from embracing her.

'Miriam!' he cried breathlessly. 'They've arrested Hephzibah!'

'I know!' As she took a step forward, Nubia saw Lupus standing behind her in the doorway.

'Lupus has just walked up from Dives's estate.' Miriam held up a wax tablet. 'And he's just written an account. There's been another murder and Nonius has accused Hephzibah! Luckily my father and Flavia and

Jonathan and Lupus arrived in time to help. Lupus stayed behind to look for clues, didn't you, Lupus?'

Gaius's big guard dog Ferox appeared in the crowded doorway. He saw Nubia dismounting from the horse and gave a single bark of greeting.

'Oh, Nubia!' cried Miriam. She followed Ferox carefully down the steps and hurried to open the gate. Lupus waved as he and Aristo followed Miriam.

'Oh, Nubia, what's happened to you?' cried Miriam. 'You're covered with blood and dirt. And you're shivering.' She took off her soft lilac palla and draped it around Nubia's shoulders. 'Senex is firing up the hot plunge for Lupus, but I think you need it more.'

Lupus nodded and held his nose and grinned at Nubia.

Miriam turned to Aristo. 'I was waiting for Gaius to return, but now that you're here . . . Can you ride to Pliny, tell him what's happened and ask him to come here at once?'

Lupus pointed eagerly at himself.

'No, Lupus,' said Miriam. 'You stay here and rest. Aristo, will you go?'

'Of course,' said Aristo and he caught the gelding's bridle.

'No.' Miriam put a hand on his arm. 'Don't take this poor creature. Can't you see he's exhausted? Take our old mule and we'll let the horse rest until after dinner. Lupus, can you give this faithful steed a good brush and a warm blanket? Good. As for you, Nubia, I think the hot plunge should be ready by now.'

An hour later – bathed and wearing one of Miriam's old lavender tunics – Nubia joined the others for dinner. It

53

was dusk. Aristo had returned with Pliny. Gaius was back from Rome, and now they were all seated in the tablinum around his wooden desk, which had been cleared of scrolls and tablets. Nubia noticed that Miriam had diplomatically placed herself between Gaius and Lupus. Nubia sat between Aristo and Pliny on the other side of the desk. Big Ferox lay faithfully at Gaius's feet and Nubia rested her bare soles on his warm back.

'Thank you, Senex,' said Miriam, as the ancient slave set a large ceramic bowl of chicken and apricot stew before them. Senex beamed at her, revealing his single tooth.

Miriam looked at Gaius. 'May I?' He nodded. Miriam pulled her palla over her head and said, 'Let us thank God.' She recited a prayer in Hebrew but finished in Latin: 'And Lord, please help Hephzibah. Come to her aid. Amen.'

While they ate, Nubia watched Miriam's husband Gaius. He was the twin brother of Flavia's father Marcus, and apart from his broken nose and a faint scar over one eyebrow, they were identical. He was a handsome man, like his brother, but almost twenty years older than his fifteen-year-old wife. Nubia thought this was very strange, and she wondered how a girl not much older than she was could love such an old man. But their love was apparent whenever they looked at each other.

'Today,' said Gaius, tearing a piece of flatbread and dipping it in the stew, 'grave events have occurred. Two men have been murdered, Hephzibah has been accused of killing them and Nubia's status has been called into question. Let's start with you, Nubia,' he said. 'Remind me: when did my brother buy you?'

'Flavia buys me last year, two days before her birthday.'

Pliny frowned. 'Flavia could not have legally bought you,' he said. 'She's still a child-in-power.'

'What is childinpower?' asked Nubia.

'A Roman father has rights over his children,' said Pliny, leaning forward. 'This is unique to us Romans. A father essentially owns his children. He also owns all they possess or acquire. He can sell or even kill his children if he wishes, though today that's frowned upon.'

Lupus grunted. When he had their attention, he pointed to Gaius, then to old Senex, emerging from the kitchen with a fresh basket of flatbread.

'Yes, Lupus,' said Pliny. 'It's very like the relationship of a master to his slaves.' He looked at Flavia's uncle. 'For example, I imagine you occasionally give that old slave money or small gifts?'

'I do,' said Gaius.

Senex nodded and showed his single tooth in a grin as he continued to shuffle forward.

Pliny turned back to Lupus and Nubia. 'Such gifts to slaves are called peculium. But even those are rightfully the owner's.'

Senex stopped in his tracks.

'Let's say that old slave were to die tonight.'

Senex gazed open-mouthed at Pliny.

'And say he'd saved up a few sesterces from what his master Gaius has given him over the years.'

Senex glanced around guiltily.

'Upon his death, that money would revert to Gaius. It rightfully belongs to him.'

A look of horror passed across Senex's face.

'At any rate, that's the law—' said Pliny and paused dramatically before adding, 'but I don't believe it's fair.'

Senex smiled with relief.

'I allow my slaves to make their own wills,' said Pliny. 'A slave like that,' here he gestured at Senex, 'could leave his few sesterces to a friend or child or fellow-slave. It's not strictly legal, but I personally wouldn't deny him that.'

Senex nodded with satisfaction, resumed his slow shuffle forward and put the basket of bread on the table.

'And as Lupus pointed out,' said Aristo, 'children are like slaves in this respect.'

'Precisely,' said Pliny. 'Male children remain in the father's power until the father dies, female children until they marry.'

'That means,' said Aristo, 'that Flavia and all her possessions actually belong to her father. Until she marries.'

'Or until her father dies,' added Pliny.

They all made the sign against evil.

'Therefore,' said Pliny to Nubia, 'you are officially the property of Marcus Flavius Geminus.'

'Could Marcus set Nubia free?' asked Miriam.

'Of course,' said Pliny, 'but he would have to do it in the presence of a magistrate. However, because Nubia is under thirty, she would not become a proper Roman citizen, as most freed slaves would.'

'She wouldn't?' said Miriam. Nubia noticed that she had hardly touched her stew.

'No. Nor would Hephzibah. I've been discussing this

with the jurists, the experts in Roman law. According to the *lex Aelia Sentia* which was instituted in the reign of Augustus, freed slaves under the age of thirty become Junian Latins.'

'What is June Latins?' asked Nubia.

'Junian Latins are essentially a type of second-class freedman, or freedwoman. They don't have all the rights of a Roman citizen like ordinary freedmen. For example, according to my jurist friend Labeo, they may own property but not dispose of it upon their death. Their property would revert to their former owner, or his official heir.' He smiled at Nubia. 'But it's still better than being a slave. Marcus can set you free tomorrow. Just make sure he gets a magistrate to witness it. Then you won't have to worry about being tortured for evidence.'

'There's only one problem,' said Aristo. 'Marcus Flavius Geminus is in Sicily, attending his patron's wedding.'

'Marcus is in Sicily?' said Gaius. 'I didn't know that.'

'Yes, you do know that, Gaius,' said Miriam gently. 'Your brother told you last week, when he brought us that nice amphora of garum.'

'Did he? I suppose I've been preoccupied.' Gaius ran his hand through his light brown hair in a gesture identical to one Flavia's father often made.

'When will he be back?' asked Pliny.

'He said not to expect him before the Nones,' said Aristo. 'At the earliest.'

Lupus grunted and pointed down.

'That's right,' said Aristo. 'Tomorrow.'

Pliny raised his rumpled eyebrows at Nubia. 'Then you'll have to remain in hiding until he returns.'

'Don't worry, Nubia.' Miriam reached out and squeezed Nubia's hand. 'We'll be happy to shelter you until Marcus returns, won't we, Gaius?'

'Of course,' said Gaius.

'And we must help poor Hephzibah.' Miriam's violet eyes filled with tears. 'She must be free to come live here. She must!' She hid her face in Gaius's shoulder and began to sob.

Gaius slipped his arm around her and kissed the top

of her head. 'Shhh, my love,' he said. 'We won't let any harm come to her.'

Miriam suddenly pushed back her chair and looked at them with liquid eyes. 'I'm sorry,' she said. 'Please excuse me.' She hurried a few paces to the bedroom and disappeared behind the curtain. They could all hear her muffled sobs.

Gaius's jaw clenched. 'Miriam's right. We've got to help Hephzibah. And we must begin by discovering the truth of what happened this afternoon at Dives's – I mean Nonius's estate.'

'I can tell you what happened immediately before she left.' Pliny tore his gaze from the bedroom curtain and looked around at them. 'You all know that Hephzibah has been staying with me since her freedom was contested. I was to be her protector and patron until her suit could be settled. After the disaster in the forum this morning – gods! was it only this morning? – I drove her straight back to my villa, only stopping to drop off Miriam. A few minutes later, a messenger arrived with a note from Nonius telling Hephzibah to pick up her things immediately, or else he would give them away. Phrixus was going back into town to do some shopping. He dropped her off and she told him she would walk back here. It doesn't take long: half an hour at most. That was the last I saw of her.'

'You should have sent someone with her,' said Aristo quietly. 'A freedman. A slave. Anyone.'

'I offered,' cried Pliny, 'but she insisted she would be fine by herself!'

'What happened next?' asked Aristo. Nubia saw him glance towards Miriam's bedroom; the sobbing had ceased.

Gaius turned to Lupus. 'According to this young man, they arrived at Dives's former estate at about the first hour after noon.'

Lupus nodded.

'The place was in turmoil,' continued Gaius. 'Hephzibah had been found crouched over a dead body. She denied the murder and Nonius was about to beat a confession out of her when Mordecai intervened. Is that correct so far, Lupus?'

Lupus grunted yes. He pretended to strike his right temple with his fist, crossed his eyes and slumped back in his chair.

'As Lupus just told us,' said Gaius, 'the victim had been killed by a single blow to his head. His name was Mercator, and he was one of Dives's freedmen. Mordecai looked for the murder weapon. But all they found was a ceramic jug.'

Lupus pointed to one of the two jugs on the table, the one containing water.

'It looked like that?' said Aristo.

Lupus nodded emphatically, then pointed inside and shook his head.

'Because it still had water in the bottom,' said Gaius, 'Lupus and the others do not believe it was the murder weapon. They also believe the crime was committed elsewhere, and Mercator's body dragged to Hephzibah's cubicle afterwards, in an attempt to implicate her.'

Lupus nodded, and then beckoned Gaius on.

'Mordecai asked Lupus to look for evidence that the crime had been committed elsewhere.'

'And did you find any such evidence, Lupus?' asked Pliny, his dark eyes bright.

Lupus nodded and held up his wax tablet. On it he had written:

SPOTS OF BLOOD IN STOREROOM NEAR SLAVE QUARTERS. LOTS OF BLUNT INSTRU-MENTS THERE, TOO.

'So Mercator probably wasn't killed in Hephzibah's cell after all,' said Pliny, 'but in the storeroom nearby. It seems there is some clever mind behind this.'

'Aristo! Lupus!' cried Flavia an hour later. 'Where have you been? We needed you! And we can't find Nubia! Jonathan and I took the dogs out into the graveyard, but we couldn't find her anywhere and now it's dark outside!'

'The rain must have washed away her scent,' said Jonathan, wheezing with anxiety. 'Nipur and I tried to track her footprints but then it got too dark—'

'We've just come from her,' said Aristo, taking off his cloak and hanging it on a wooden peg of the vestibule, 'and she's perfectly safe. I found her at Avita's tomb this afternoon, and I took her to stay with Miriam and your Uncle Gaius.'

'Oh, praise Juno!' sobbed Flavia. 'Thank you, Aristo. Thank you for finding Nubia.'

He nodded grimly. 'Lupus and I have just had dinner there,' he said. 'We heard all about the second murder.'

Lupus looked up from patting the dogs and nodded.

'Oh, Aristo!' cried Flavia. 'I saw two dead bodies today. It was horrible.'

'I know. Death is a horrible thing.' He looked around the atrium. 'Where is Hephzibah? Nubia and I were watching from the woods when you passed by in the carruca. We saw the vigiles had her in custody. Miriam hoped she would be under Mordecai's protection.'

Flavia shook her head. 'They put her in a horrible little cell behind the basilica.'

'We can't get the vadimonium until tomorrow,' explained Jonathan. 'Father has gone to take her blankets.'

Flavia shivered and pulled her palla tighter round her shoulders. 'It's going to be cold tonight. Oh, but I'm so glad Nubia is all right.' She bent and took Nipur's head in her hands. 'Nubia's safe! Your mistress is in good hands.'

'Yes,' said Aristo. 'She's in very good hands, so don't worry. 'Come. Let's go into the tablinum. I want you to tell me again exactly what happened this afternoon.'

Last will and testament of Jonathan ben Mordecai.

I doubt that anybody will ever find this or read it. And even if they do, I've probably done it wrong and so it will be invalid. But I don't suppose it will matter because I'll be dead.

Here is a list of my possessions and the people who should get them.

any money I might have	*my mother and father*
my dog Tigris	*Nubia*
my hunting things (bow, arrows, etc.)	*Lupus*
my clothes and shoes	*ditto*
my small collection of scrolls	*Flavia Gemina*
my herb pouch	*Polla Pulchra*

Everything else should be given to the poor or thrown away

(I have written this because I keep dreaming about a funeral procession and I think it's mine.)

Written – but not sealed or witnessed – the day before the Nones of December in the consulship of Titus Caesar Vespasian Augustus and Domitian Caesar.

Miriam had made a bed of blankets for Nubia in a corner of Gaius's small tablinum. It was soft and warm, but without Nipur's comforting bulk at her feet she found it hard to sleep. Somewhere in the woods outside the lodge an owl hooted his mournful cry and later she heard the squeal of its prey. A mouse. Or perhaps a shrew. She remembered the tiny corpse she had buried earlier that day, and how completely lifeless it had been. What was the spark that made creatures live? Was it the breath of God, as Jonathan's family believed? Or something else?

The owl cried again further away and she was finally drifting off to sleep when Ferox's deep warning bark brought her wide awake and set her heart racing. Then she heard it: a soft, urgent knock on the front door. They had come for her in the dead of night, when there was no escape!

From Miriam and Gaius's bedroom came a thump and a curse, and the sound of Gaius shushing Ferox and then the knock came again, softly. Three raps, a pause, then three raps again.

Nubia heard Miriam's voice, urgent and insisting, then the skitter of Ferox's toenails on the pebbled walkway and his excited panting. A moment later came Miriam's whisper, close-at-hand.

'Nubia! I don't think it's the vigiles, but stay

absolutely still and silent. Be ready to run to your hiding place.'

Nubia nodded, even though she knew Miriam couldn't see her in the darkness. Her heart was pounding like a rabbit's.

From between the legs of the desk Nubia caught a glimpse of Miriam's heavily pregnant form, dimly lit by the small oil lamp in her hand.

The sound of the bar being slid across, a few urgent whispers, then Miriam called: 'I have to go out, Gaius. Will you drive me?'

'Great Neptune's beard, woman!' came his muffled voice from the bedroom. Then, louder as he came into the courtyard: 'It's not one of your wretched women again, is it?'

'It's Lydia, up at the estate of Barbillus.'

'Can't she send for your father?'

'Too far. The baby is coming now. Gaius, please. She needs me. She knows me. I've been attending her.'

'But it's almost your time, too. You shouldn't be going out in the middle of the night to deliver babies.'

'Gaius. She's frightened. She needs me.'

'All right,' his voice was low. 'I'll drive you.'

'Thank you, my love.'

'Come on, Ferox! Here, boy! Now, where are those useless slaves?'

'No, don't wake them. They're fast asleep.'

'Wretched creatures,' he grumbled. Nubia heard the front door open wide. A moment later a cold draft caressed her cheek and brought in the scent of the vineyard. She heard Ferox panting happily: he and his master were going on a night adventure! The excited panting receded and after a short pause, Nubia heard Miriam's voice from the tablinum doorway.

'Nubia, Gaius and I are going out. A woman at a nearby estate is about to give birth. Shall I wake Dromo or Senex and have them keep watch?'

'No,' whispered Nubia. 'I am not afraid.'

But afterwards, she wished she had at least asked for Ferox. For when they left the house silent and dark, and the owl began to hoot again, Nubia found herself trembling violently. And she did not fall asleep until Gaius and Miriam returned at dawn.

'Oh!' groaned Flavia the next morning. 'Why doesn't Caudex open the front door? Someone's been banging on it for ages.'

She covered her head with a pillow but the knocking continued.

A moment later she pulled off the pillow, rolled over and opened her eyes. Scuto and Nipur were nowhere to be seen, Nubia's bed was empty and had not been slept in.

Suddenly it all came flooding back.

Nubia was hiding at her uncle's house, Hephzibah was in a prison cell and her father was in Sicily.

Or was he? Today was the Nones and he'd said he might be back by then. Once again came the urgent pounding on the front door.

'Pater!' Flavia scrambled out of bed, pulled off the blue blanket, wrapped it around her like a palla and hurried downstairs.

But it was not her father at the door; it was Pliny.

'Good news and bad, Flavia Gemina,' he said, taking a single step into the vestibule. 'The good news is that they're going to try Hephzibah's case in our own basilica, right here in Ostia. The bad news is that the date is set for the day after tomorrow; seven days before the Ides.'

'The day after tomorrow? Why is that bad news?' said Flavia, and called over her shoulder, 'Alma? Caudex?'

'It's bad news because it's terribly short notice. It also means I won't be able to defend her. I have to go to Rome for a few days. Urgent business.'

'Our slaves must both be out shopping.' Flavia looked around the atrium. 'Or maybe Alma's walking the dogs. And I can't imagine where Aristo—' she looked at Pliny in alarm. 'You can't defend Hephzibah?'

'Unfortunately not.' He had not followed her into the atrium, but remained standing just inside the doorway. 'I'm on my way to Rome now. Urgent business. But I wanted to tell you as soon as possible. And to give you this.' He held out an official-looking wax tablet.

Flavia moved back to the doorway and took the tablet from his outstretched hand. 'What's this?'

'Details of the case. Time, place, formula, magistrate presiding and so on. You should give it to whoever decides to defend her.'

'But who? Who can defend her?'

'I don't know.' Pliny stepped back over the threshold so that he was outside again. 'Your uncle, perhaps? Or your tutor?'

'I don't think Uncle Gaius has studied rhetoric. And Aristo isn't a Roman citizen. He's Greek. Can a non-Roman citizen plead in court?'

'I'm sorry, Flavia.' Pliny gestured vaguely up Green Fountain Street in the direction of the Roman Gate.

'My carruca's waiting for me. I must go. Good luck!' he called over his shoulder.

Flavia gazed open-mouthed until he was out of sight.

SCROLL VIII

'Flavia!' called Jonathan. 'Why are you standing in the road with messy hair and a blanket wrapped around you?'

Flavia turned to see Jonathan coming down the street with his father and Lupus and Tigris. Copper-haired Hephzibah was with them, too, looking pale and tired.

'Have you only just got up?' continued Jonathan. 'It's already the second hour!'

'Is it?' She stooped to stroke Tigris, then stood up again. 'Pliny was just here. He gave me this.'

'Peace be with you, Flavia,' said Mordecai, and gave his little bow. 'As you see, we've just collected Hephzibah from the cells of the basilica.'

'Good morning, Hephzibah,' said Flavia. 'Was it awful there?'

Hephzibah gave a small shake of her head. Flavia saw she was shivering, although it was a sunny morning, and mild for December.

Flavia gave Hephzibah an encouraging smile. 'Are you going back to Miriam's now?'

'No,' said Mordecai. 'I want Hephzibah to stay here with us until the trial. It's more convenient for her to be here in town. Are those the details of the trial?'

'Yes.' Flavia showed him the tablet. 'Seven days before the Ides. The day after tomorrow.'

'Master of the Universe! That won't give young Pliny much time to prepare.'

'Doctor Mordecai! Pliny can't defend Hephzibah after all. He has urgent business in Rome.'

'Oh dear,' said Mordecai. 'Oh dear. That is grave news indeed.'

'Can't *you* defend her, father?' asked Jonathan.

'No, my son,' said Mordecai. 'I have very little knowledge of the procedure in Roman law courts, and even less of rhetoric.' He looked at Flavia. 'Perhaps your uncle?'

'Good idea!' said Flavia, and her eyes lit up. 'We'll go to Laurentum to ask Uncle Gaius to defend Hephzibah, and at the same time we can see Nubia. May we go to Laurentum, Doctor Mordecai?'

He sighed and nodded. 'Very well, but take the dogs to protect you.'

'Good idea,' she said. 'As soon as Alma brings Scuto and Nipur back, we'll take all the dogs to Laurentum and leave Nipur to comfort Nubia.' She looked at Jonathan and Lupus. 'Aristo's nowhere to be seen, so he can't complain that we didn't turn up for lessons. How do you both fancy a nice long walk?'

'Great Jupiter's eyebrows!' muttered Flavia's uncle Gaius an hour and a half later. 'I can't defend Hephzibah! I have no training.'

It was a glorious morning, more like late autumn than early winter. The four children and their dogs were having a late breakfast in the tablinum of the Laurentum Lodge. Miriam and Gaius were both pale

69

and tired; they had been up all night attending a childbirth. Nubia looked tired, too, but she had been overjoyed to see her friends and her dog Nipur, who now panted happily at his mistress's feet.

'Oh, Gaius, you have to defend Hephzibah!' said Miriam. 'If you don't, who will?'

'I don't know,' said Gaius. 'But I can't do it. I've never studied rhetoric, not properly. It takes years to master the skill.'

'Who do we know who *has* studied rhetoric?' said Jonathan through a mouthful of porridge.

'I know!' cried Flavia suddenly. 'I know who might do it!'

'Tell us, Flavia,' said her uncle, stifling a yawn. 'Who?'

'No.' Flavia's shoulders slumped and she shook her head. 'It's a silly idea. I don't know if he's in Rome. Or even in the country.'

'By all the gods, Flavia!' cried Gaius. 'Give me his name and I'll ride into Rome right now.'

'But he might not be at home,' said Flavia. 'The odds are a hundred to one.'

'And what about your olive harvest?' said Miriam.

'I'll take the odds he's there,' said her uncle.

'Do you have something I can write on?' asked Flavia, and added, 'So that I can write him a quick note?'

Lupus held up his wax tablet, but Gaius leant back in his chair and plucked a sheet of papyrus from a shelf. He passed the papyrus to Flavia, then handed her an inkwell and quill pen, and she began to write. Presently she wrote an address on the back of the papyrus, folded it and accepted a lit candle from her uncle. She dripped some wax on the place where the edges overlapped, then pressed her signet-ring into the glob of liquid wax. As she waited for it to dry, she looked up at her friends. They were all staring at her.

'Can't you think who I mean?' she asked them.

They all shook their heads and Lupus gave her his bug-eyed look and an exaggerated shrug, as if to say: 'Who?'

Flavia smiled. 'You'll find out soon enough,' she said. But her smile faded as she handed the papyrus note to her uncle: '*If* he's there. And *if* he accepts.'

When Flavia and the boys returned home an hour later, they found Aristo pacing back and forth in the atrium.

'I've spent all morning in the forum,' he said, after they told him their news. 'Trying to find out more about Papillio and Mercator, the two murdered men.'

'What did you discover?' asked Flavia. 'Did they know Hephzibah?'

'As far as I could discover: no. There is no connection between either of them and Hephzibah. In fact, neither of them seem to have anything in common, apart from the fact that they both knew Hephzibah's former master, Dives. I'm going back into town and find out everything I can about him; about Dives, I mean.' He took his cloak from its peg and then turned to look at them.

'You three may go to the baths this afternoon,' he said. 'But nowhere else. No more charging off to Laurentum, as you did this morning.'

'But Doctor Mordecai told us we could go. Besides,' added Flavia, 'now that we've rid Ostia of kidnappers, it's perfectly safe to walk around town.'

'Flavia. Yesterday there were two brutal murders

within a five-mile radius of this house. I don't want you to be next. While your father is away you are my responsibility.'

'May we at least go to Jonathan's?'

Aristo rolled his eyes. 'Of course you may go next door. But be sensible. I'll be back in time for dinner. Probably sooner.'

'We'll be sensible,' said Flavia and waited for the door to close behind him. Then she turned to the boys. 'Good. He's gone. Let's go investigate.'

'Where?' said Jonathan.

'Next door, to your house, of course. It's time we had a long talk with Hephzibah.'

'She's resting in Miriam's old room,' said Jonathan's mother Susannah. 'I don't think the poor girl got much sleep in that cold cell last night. I promised to take her to the baths when they open, but I'll see if she's happy to come down and speak to you first.'

Flavia nodded and stared at Susannah. Jonathan's mother rarely spent time with her family. She occupied her days either wandering the streets of Ostia or weaving in the privacy of her bedroom, which was separate from her husband's.

'We'll wait in the dining room,' said Jonathan.

Susannah smiled at him, and touched his cheek, then turned to go upstairs.

Flavia followed the boys into Jonathan's triclinium. It was the same size and shape as hers, but it felt very different. The plaster-covered walls were a deep cinnabar-red. Winter carpets of red, blue, gold and purple covered the black and white mosaic floor. Richly embroidered cushions and bolsters surrounded a low octagonal table of dark wood inlaid with mother-of-pearl.

Flavia closed her eyes and inhaled the pleasant scent of cinnamon, mint and cumin.

Presently Susannah brought Hephzibah into the dining room. The slave-girl looked pale but rested in a cream stola. Her magnificent auburn hair was netted but unpinned and Flavia saw that it reached halfway down her back.

'I'll ask Delilah to bring you all some sage tea and sesame cakes,' said Susannah, and then added, 'Be gentle with Hephzibah. So much has happened in the past few days.'

'Yes,' murmured Flavia. 'So much *has* happened in the past few days.' She looked up at Hephzibah and patted the scarlet bolster next to her. 'Come, Hephzibah. Sit. We need you to help us, so that we can help you. Tell us about your life. Tell us everything.'

'I was born in Jerusalem, in the reign of Nero, one year before the Great Revolt in Judaea.' Hephzibah was sitting cross-legged on a cushion, sipping hot sage tea. 'They say I was born on a portentous day: the ninth of Av.'

'The day the First Temple was destroyed,' murmured Jonathan.

'And the Second Temple, too,' said Hephzibah in her low, accented voice. 'I turned five on the day they burned God's House. I remember my father had taken me to a place where there might be food. He wanted me to have something to eat on my birthday. But when we got there, we found the food had all gone. I cried and cried; I had set my heart on a persimmon.'

'What's a persimmon?' asked Flavia.

'It's a fruit like an apple,' said Jonathan, 'but with a shiny orange skin, and softer.'

Hephzibah sipped her tea. 'The Jews had burned all the persimmon groves outside the city, to stop them falling into Roman hands, and all the trees in the city had been stripped long before. By this time the famine was very bad.' Hephzibah set her beaker on the octagonal table and continued.

'Father lifted me up in his arms and carried me back home. That was when we stopped to watch the Temple portico burn. I will never forget the sight of the Romans running like ants up on the flaming portico. Most of those watching lamented to see God's Temple burn, but some cheered to see Roman soldiers on fire.'

Beside Flavia, Jonathan groaned and hid his face in his hands.

Hephzibah continued. 'Suddenly everyone grew silent. One Roman soldier was calling out to his comrades below. We could not hear his words, but we could guess what he was saying. He was trapped on the upper level, with the flames almost upon him. Then a Roman on the lower level ran forward and held out his arms. I will never forget that. It was a huge drop, but that Roman held out his arm to his friend.'

'What happened?'

'The first Roman jumped and the second one caught him. The man who jumped got up, but I think the one who tried to catch him was killed. I often wonder what happened to those two men. They must have been good friends for one to give his life for the other. I often wonder, because before we reached home, a fellow Jew – one of our own – attacked my father and killed him.

The man killed my father for his leather belt. I think he wanted to eat it.'

'Oh!' cried Flavia.

'My father died in my arms,' said Hephzibah. 'With his last breath he prayed that the Eternal One would protect me.'

Out of the corner of her eye Flavia saw a small movement. Lupus's fists clenching and unclenching. Jonathan's head was still down.

'When I led my mother to my father's body,' said Hephzibah, 'she collapsed and became delirious and nearly died. Later, when the Romans came they took one look at her and tossed her onto a pile of dead bodies. I went to lie beside her, there among the corpses, not knowing if she was alive or dead, not knowing whether *I* was alive or dead.'

Hephzibah took a sip of sweet sage tea and closed her eyes. 'We did not die,' she continued presently, 'nor were we put in chains, like the thousands of others. At the time we thought this is a blessing. Later we knew we would have been better off if we had been sold as slaves.'

'Better off as slaves?' Jonathan raised his head and looked at her in amazement.'

'Yes,' said Hephzibah. 'My grandfather Eleazar – my mother's father – was one of a small group of rebels taking shelter in the desert. They had occupied a stronghold, a place where even the Romans could not reach us. My mother decided we should go to him. It took us many days and we overcame many hardships. But at last we reached our refuge.'

'Oh no,' said Jonathan, his dark eyes wide. 'You didn't go *there*, did you?'

'Yes,' said Hephzibah. 'We went there.'

Once again, Jonathan hid his face in his hands and groaned.

Flavia and Lupus exchanged a glance of alarm.

'Where?' asked Flavia. 'Where did you go?'

'Herod's great stronghold,' said Hephzibah, and looked at Flavia with anguished eyes: 'Masada.'

SCROLL IX

'Masada?' said Flavia. 'Who's Masada?'

Jonathan lifted his head from his hands. 'Not who,' he said, 'where.'

'Masada was a barren mountain, rising up in the Judaean desert,' said Hephzibah. 'Then Herod built a magnificent palace there, with terraced gardens and living quarters and underground cisterns for unlimited water. It is in the heart of the fiercest desert known to man. From its highest tower you can see twenty miles in any direction, when the heat does not shimmer like an oven. Masada means "fortress" in our language. It was designed so that it could never be captured. It was impregnable. Invincible. Unassailable. My mother and I were there for three years. Then the Romans took it.'

Nubia was in the tiny kitchen of the Laurentum Lodge, helping Miriam grind chestnut flour, when Nipur lifted his head from his paws and pricked his ears and growled. A moment later they heard Ferox's deep bark coming from the vestibule.

Miriam glanced at Nubia, then wiped her hands on a cloth and turned towards the front door. 'It can't be Gaius,' she murmured. 'Ferox never barks at Gaius.'

Before she had taken a single step they heard the pounding on the door.

'Go, Nubia!' whispered Miriam. 'Out the back door. Go to the place we prepared for you! I will send them away if I can.'

Nipur was on his feet now so Nubia crouched and took his big head between her hands and said, 'Stay!'

Then she quietly opened the kitchen door and ran to her hiding place.

'Masada was impregnable,' said Hephzibah, 'and yet the Romans managed to take it. It took them an entire year to build a ramp, but only one week to breach the wall. When they finally broke through, they discovered our people had built another wall. This inner wall was made of wood and earth. The Romans tried using their battering ram. But its blows only packed the loose earth more tightly, and made it stronger.

'Late that afternoon, the Romans realised they could burn our inner wall, because it was partly wood. They put the torches to it and we groaned as the last barrier between us and them caught fire. Then we cheered: the Lord had changed the wind and made it blow flames back upon the Romans. In their eagerness to escape, they trampled each other and many fell from the ramp.

'But the miraculous wind did not last. As the first stars appeared in the sky, the evening breeze arose and turned the flames back towards us. We watched the wall burn, our hearts dying within us. It was dusk and the Romans were retreating, but we knew they would finish the job – and us – at dawn the next morning. Their legions surrounded us. There was no escape.

'That night our men stayed up late, debating what to

do. My mother told me to watch some other children in her care, children without parents whom she had taken under her wing. She wanted to find out what the leaders intended to do. Their meeting was secret, but she knew a place from which she could listen and not be seen.'

Jonathan stared at Hephzibah but she did not seem to notice. She continued: 'We children were terrified of the Romans. We had all heard stories of what the Romans did to their prisoners. The other children were all younger, so I had to be in charge. I was eight. I told them stories to comfort them. My mother was a long, long time. She was so long that I began to be frightened that maybe the Romans had crept in by night and killed her. All the other children were fast asleep by now.'

Hephzibah finished her sage tea.

'Finally my mother returned. She had an old lady with her – Anna – who spent all her days in prayer. I always thought she was mad to do nothing but pray. I was about to ask my mother why she had brought a madwoman, when I saw that she was weeping. That was the first time I saw her weep since she had found my father's body. Finally she dried her tears and woke the children, for by now it was after midnight. Mother made us all rise and dress ourselves and then she led us in silence along dark paths to the furthest cistern of the aqueduct that Herod had built. Old Anna came, too.

'We were all very frightened, expecting the Romans to leap out of the shadows and cut our throats. Finally we reached the cistern and went carefully down stairs carved out of the rock itself. For a while the moon gave us a little filtered light, milky blue in the cistern. Then it set, and we were plunged into darkness.

'That was the longest night I have ever known. But at last it began to grow light and we heard faint cockcrow. Not long after that came the distant shouts of the Roman commander, and the faint crash of the wall being destroyed. We braced ourselves for the sounds of men yelling and swords clashing and walls tumbling down. But there was nothing. Utter silence. For one hour, two, three, six. Presently we could tell by the bright blue light that it must be noon. The youngest of the children was very hungry. I remember his name was Zechariah. He began to cry and we could not comfort him.

'Then we heard footsteps, the distinctive crunch of the metal studs on the soles of their boots. We hugged each other and whimpered. At last they appeared in the blue-lit doorway. Two Roman soldiers. One had a limp. The other was very young and handsome and I will never forget what happened next.'

'What happened next?' whispered Flavia.

'Those two Roman soldiers began to weep and praise the gods and the young one took each one of us in his arms and kissed the top of our heads. Even mother. Even old Anna.'

Lupus was frowning and he made his 'Why?' grunt.

'He was so happy to see us alive,' said Hephzibah. 'You see, all the other Jews in Masada were dead.'

Flavia and Lupus stared at her in horror. Jonathan's head was down.

'How?' said Flavia.

'They had committed mass suicide,' said Hephzibah. 'Each husband had gently cut the throats of his wife and children, then a man chosen by lot had killed each of them.'

'What?' gasped Flavia. 'All of them?'

Hephzibah nodded. 'Of nearly one thousand people, we seven were the only ones still alive.'

Between the stables and the vineyard of the Laurentum Lodge was an ancient wine press. It was a rectangular stone tank, with three lions' head spouts low on one side. All over Italia – in the months of September and October – half-naked slaves would tread grapes in tanks like this one, their bare legs stained purple to mid-thigh and the juice gushing out of the lions' mouths into wide clay bowls. From there it would be strained into wooden barrels and allowed to ferment.

The previous day, Gaius and Dromo had constructed a false bottom to the press by hammering a few planks together and resting it on bricks. Then they had spread this false bottom with sticky grey birdlime and covered it with a layer of grapes. When it was in place, it made the wine press appear to be half-full of grapes ready for the treading.

Now, with shaking hands, Nubia lifted the false bottom and climbed into the press and let the low table slip back in place above her. She hoped none of the grapes would roll away from the sticky birdlime to expose the wood underneath.

She pressed her cheek against the rough stone floor of the press and inhaled the faint scent of mouldy grapeskins. The lions' head spouts allowed a little light to filter in so that it was not pitch black. Nubia wriggled forward and pressed her eye to one of the spouts. She could just see the olive tree at the corner of the Lodge and the path at the end of the vine rows. Even as she looked, the four-toothed slave Dromo shuffled into sight, carrying a basket full of grapes. He came so close that for a moment his leg blocked the light from her spout. Then he stepped to one side and the light streamed in and a hundred little thuds rained down above her as he emptied the basket of grapes into the press.

Then she heard another sound, one that chilled her blood: it was the clink of armour.

'Search the stables, Decimus!' she heard a man call. 'I'll have a look over here. What are you up to, grandpa?'

Nubia's heart thudded. It was the vigiles! They were searching for her! For a moment she closed her eyes, not daring to look, then she allowed herself a peep. And gasped. She could see part of the soldiers' hairy, muscular calf. He was standing right beside the press.

'Where's your master, old man?'

'Rome,' quavered Dromo. 'Master's up in Rome.'

'Bit late in the year to be treading grapes, isn't it?' said the soldier, and she heard Dromo mumble an apology.

Then the lion's head spout peephole showed her something which made her heart stutter.

Her dog Nipur had appeared from the direction of the Lodge and was trotting up the path, straight towards her. He was panting happily and wagging his tail.

Horrified, Nubia watched him coming closer and closer until his sniffing black nose blocked out the light.

'No, Nipur!' she cried out in her mind. 'Flee! You'll give away my hiding place!'

SCROLL X

'After the soldiers found us,' said Hephzibah, 'they led us up out of the aqueduct. The only way back was through a courtyard. When we entered they warned us not to look, but to keep our eyes downcast. But I peeked. I wish I had listened to them.'

'Why?' breathed Flavia. 'What did you see?'

Hephzibah hung her head. 'I saw some of the bodies. In their dying moments the mothers wrapped their arms around their children. And the fathers had embraced their wives. And their blood had mingled on the tiles of the courtyard.'

They were all quiet for a moment. Presently Hephzibah said, in little more than a whisper, 'That sight will haunt me for the rest of my life.'

'Yes,' said Jonathan, his voice barely audible. 'I know.'

'What happened then?' asked Flavia. 'After the Romans captured you?'

'We were brought here to Italia, for the triumph,' said Hephzibah. 'I don't remember it very well. I was so ill on the boat that they thought I might die. But I didn't die. And in the end they didn't bother to execute us. We were only two women and five little children.

Eventually we were bought by one of the Emperor's freedmen, a man called Titus Flavius Josephus.'

'Josephus!' said Flavia. 'A Jew with a bushy black beard? The man writing the history of the Jewish Rebellion?'

'Yes,' said Hephzibah. 'He wanted to talk to us, to listen to our accounts of the sieges of Jerusalem and Masada. He spent many hours with my mother and old Anna. And three times he interviewed me, too. I was only eight or perhaps nine by then, but I remembered everything. Whenever he finished questioning me, he would reward me with a honey cake or an almond-stuffed date. I suppose Josephus finally got what he wanted from us, because a month or two after he bought us, he sold me and my mother to a Syrian carpet-maker with a workshop on the Esquiline Hill. We worked there for over five years, but the master's health failed and eventually his business, too. He sold us at auction last winter. And that,' she concluded, 'is when Dives bought me and my mother.'

Final will of Nubia Shepenwepet daughter of Nastasen of the leopard clan.

Even though I belong to Marcus Flavius Geminus sea captain and all my possessions are his I wish to give to people I love. If Captain Geminus permits I make his daughter Flavia Gemina to be my heir. To her I leave my portion of gold for finding racehorse Sagitta. I also leave my tiger-eye earrings as memory of me.

To Aristo I give flute my most precious possession. Dear Aristo whenever you play it to imagine I kiss you and remember I love you always for ever.

To friend Jonathan who makes me to laugh I give Nipur

brother to Tigris. Take care of him. He was precious to me.

To friend Lupus who makes me also to laugh, I give jade bracelet or arm-guard. It is Green reward for helping them.

To Alma who shows love by food I give my hairpins, oils and unguents.

To Caudex who shows love by protecting I give my lionskin cloak to use it for soft blanket.

My life was full of love and loss also, but at the last was love and for this I rejoice. Please promise my ashes to be placed in Geminus family tomb with the ashes of Flavia one day close beside me.

Witnessed by Nipur – see pawprint in wax – who almost betrays me today the Nones of December. He does not mean to betray but makes me realise life to be short and that one day I die perhaps by surprise and that I should therefore write this.

'We have to solve this mystery,' said Flavia later that afternoon, 'so that we can help Hephzibah. The poor thing has suffered so much.'

They had been to the baths, and now the three of them were sitting in Flavia's bedroom, watching Scuto and Tigris wrestle good-naturedly on the floor.

'I've been thinking about this case—' began Flavia, then paused as Lupus grunted and held his right finger before his lips. They all listened and Flavia could faintly hear a man's shouting voice.

'It's the town crier,' said Jonathan. 'He only goes through the streets when the news is important.'

'Shhh!' said Flavia. 'Quiet, Scuto! Quiet, Tigris!'

Praeco was at least three streets away, but if they were quiet they could hear his words perfectly:

'TWO BLOODY MURDERS COMMITTED!' came his distant cry. 'ONE IN OSTIA, ONE IN LAURENTUM. IF ANYONE HAS INFORMATION ABOUT THESE KILLINGS, PLEASE REPORT TO THE BASILICA.' His voice grew fainter, he must have turned a corner. 'A REWARD OF ONE THOUSAND SESTERCES IS OFFERED BY THE ILLUSTRIOUS AND GENEROUS LUCIUS NONIUS CELER FOR ANY INFORMATION ABOUT THE PROFANE MURDERS OF GNAEUS HELVIUS PAPILLIO AND GAIUS ARTORIUS MERCATOR. TWO BLOODY MURDERS . . .'

Now his voice had faded, so Flavia turned to Jonathan and Lupus. 'I've been thinking about this case,' she said again, 'and I've been mentally listing everything we know. Here's what I've come up with. Let me know if I've missed anything.'

On Nubia's bed, the boys nodded and Lupus took out his wax tablet. The dogs resumed their tussle.

'Fifteen years ago in Jerusalem,' began Flavia, 'Hephzibah is born into a highborn Jewish family. Her father is a priest and her mother's father a Zealot, maybe even a sicarius. Hephzibah survives the destruction of Jerusalem and the terrible mass-suicide of Masada and at the age of eight is sold into slavery with her mother. For six years they serve in Rome. Then they are put up for auction and bought by a rich man called Dives, who once served as a soldier in Judaea. Hephzibah and her mother come to his Laurentum estate just before the Saturnalia. Almost exactly one year ago.'

Scuto yelped as Tigris's playful nipping got too rough. Jonathan pulled his dog away from Flavia's, and began searching his fur for ticks. 'I hope Aristo finds out more about Dives,' he said.

'Me, too,' said Flavia and absently stroked Scuto. 'At Dives's estate, Hephzibah works as a seamstress and her

87

mother as a laundress. But less than two months after they go to live there, Hephzibah's mother dies of the fever.'

'The one that nearly killed all of us,' said Jonathan, without looking up from Tigris's fur.

Flavia nodded. 'Ten months later, Dives suddenly decides to set Hephzibah free. He does so in great secrecy, in the presence of a magistrate called Papillio. Hephzibah remembers that a wax tablet was duly signed and sealed, but no trace of this tablet has yet been found.

'Three days after Dives frees Hephzibah, he dies. This is not unexpected. He has been an invalid for many years and is very fat.'

'But,' continued Jonathan, 'according to a Jewish freedwoman named Restituta, there's a rumour among the slaves that he was murdered.'

'That could be crucial,' said Flavia. 'Lupus, can you make a note of that? It's another thing we must investigate. Especially as Nonius has now accused Hephzibah of murdering Dives.'

Lupus nodded and bent his head over his tablet.

'After Dives's death,' continued Flavia, 'his heir comes to take over the estate. Nonius is about twenty-five years old. Hephzibah tells Nonius she is free, and therefore not his property, but she cannot remember the name of the man who witnessed her manumission, and there seems to be no record of it. She asks her friend Miriam to find the witness. Miriam asks us. We find out the witness is Papillio. Pliny sends him a summons to appear before the magistrate to testify that Hephzibah is free. But then Papillio is found dying from a stab wound, and he utters the cryptic last words: *I didn't tell. Quick. Find the other six. By Hercules.*'

'The question is what *other six*?' said Jonathan.

Lupus nodded his agreement.

'I don't have a clue,' said Flavia, and continued: 'Later that day Nonius tells Hephzibah to come and collect her possessions, or he will give them away. She arrives a short time later, clutching a bag of gold from Miriam. She later tells us that she wanted to buy her freedom.'

'And yet the first thing she does,' said Jonathan with a frown, 'is to visit a friend . . . what was her name?'

'Priscilla,' said Flavia: 'a pregnant kitchen slave. Hephzibah claims she looked for Nonius, but couldn't find him. *Then* she goes to collect her things, and that is when she finds a dead body in her cubicle: one of Dives's freedmen, a merchant named Mercator. Hephzibah knows him by sight, but claims never to have spoken to him or had any dealings with him. Furthermore, there are no traces of blood or a struggle in her cubicle, whereas drops of blood were noted in a storeroom nearby.'

Lupus gave a little bow.

'Therefore,' concluded Flavia, 'it seems that someone is trying to implicate her in the murders. But who?' she murmured. 'And why?'

'I think we need to find out more about the pregnant slave-girl Priscilla,' said Jonathan. 'And—'

'Flavia?' interrupted a voice from the doorway. Alma stood there, wiping her hands on her apron.

Flavia and the others looked up at her, surprised.

'There's a young man downstairs,' said Alma. 'A very handsome young man. And judging by the crescent buckles on his boots and the broad stripes on his tunic, he's of the senatorial class. Is there something you want to tell your old nursemaid?'

Flavia looked at Alma blankly. Then her face lit up and she clapped her hands. 'Euge!' she cried. 'It's him! Praise Juno!'

'Who?' said Jonathan, and exchanged a puzzled glance with Lupus.

'Our saviour!'

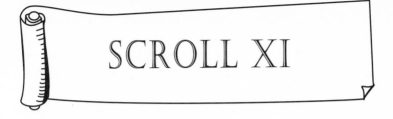

SCROLL XI

He was waiting for them in the atrium: tall, dark and patrician. An old man stood behind him, carrying a scroll case in one hand and a leather travelling bag in the other.

The young man was leaning forward to examine a fresco on the wall – a scene of Castor and Pollux – and he was chewing his usual mastic gum. When he heard their footsteps he turned and squinted and then gave Flavia a heart-stopping smile.

'Floppy!' squealed Flavia, and almost rushed to hug him. Then she remembered herself and flushed, 'I mean: welcome, Gaius Valerius Flaccus,' she said in a more dignified tone. 'Thank you so much for coming.'

'Hello, Flavia. Jonathan. Lupus,' said Flaccus, his voice deep and cultured. 'How are you all?'

Lupus gave Flaccus a thumbs-up and pointed back with raised eyebrows.

'I'm well, too, thank you.' Flaccus took off a dusty blue travelling cloak and handed it to the old man, apparently his slave. 'I've only just returned from Halicarnassus.'

At the mention of 'Halicarnassus' Flavia exchanged a glance with Lupus and Jonathan. They had met Flaccus the previous spring on a voyage to Rhodes and he had helped them rescue kidnapped children. They suspected a criminal mastermind who was based in Halicarnassus.

'No sailing this late in the year,' Flaccus was saying in his velvety voice, 'so we had to come overland from Brundisium. It took us nearly a month. I only arrived in Rome yesterday and I hadn't even started to go through all the letters waiting for me when your uncle arrived.' Flaccus laughed, showing even white teeth. 'At first I was very confused. I took him for your father.'

'They're twins,' said Flavia with a laugh, aware that her heart was pounding.

'So I discovered. Anyway, Gaius told me your problem and he begged me to help.'

'Oh, Flaccus!' cried Flavia, 'We're begging, too. The trial is the day after tomorrow and we have nobody to help us. You can sleep in our guestroom and use pater's tablinum to prepare your case. We'll feed you and do research for you and Aristo can be your assistant in court. Just please say you'll defend Hephzibah. You're our only hope!'

Gaius Valerius Flaccus smiled. 'Of course I'll defend her,' he said. 'That's why I'm here.'

'*Amicus certus in re incerta cernitur,*' said a voice and they all turned to look at the old man standing behind Flaccus. 'A friend in need is a friend indeed,' said the old man with a wink.

Flaccus grinned. 'Flavia, Jonathan, Lupus: this is Lynceus. He was pater's scribe and secretary, and now he's mine. He's slightly deaf, but makes up for it with his keen vision. And you'll find he has a motto for almost every occasion.'

'Cicero, quoting Ennius,' said Lynceus, and gave

them another wink. He was short and balding with an intelligent twinkle in his eye. Flavia liked him.

'Welcome to you both,' she said. 'Shall I ask Alma to make you some spiced wine? Or would you rather I show you to the guest room?'

Flaccus shook his head and grinned. 'First things first,' he said. 'Please will you point us in the right direction of Ostia's best bath-house?'

'Jonathan!' said Flavia, coming into the small guest room. 'This is Flaccus's room now. And he'll be back from the baths any minute.'

Jonathan was sitting on the freshly made-up bed and laughing. He held a papyrus scroll in his hand. 'Flavia, you have to see this. It's Lupus the rhetor.' He pointed with his chin. Flavia turned to see Lupus standing in a corner of the room. He had draped a red-bordered toga around himself and was staring nobly into the middle distance with his right arm upraised in the classic gesture of an orator asking for silence.

'Lupus! That's one of Floppy's togas! Take it off immediately!'

Lupus merely raised one eyebrow and looked down his nose at her, cross-eyed.

Jonathan giggled. 'Watch this,' he said, and read from the scroll. *'One of the commonest of all the gestures consists in placing the middle finger against the thumb and extending the remaining three: it is suitable to the exordium. Move the hand forward with an easy motion both to right and left, while the head and shoulders gradually follow the direction of the gesture.'*

In his corner, Lupus adopted the gesture and swung his arm easily back and forth.

'It is also useful in the statement of facts, but if we are reproaching our adversary, the same movement may be employed with vehemence and energy.'

Lupus swung his arm more vigorously, over-balanced, stepped on the hem of his overlong toga and almost pitched face forward. He caught himself and adopted an air of insulted dignity.

Flavia couldn't help grinning. 'He looks like a small but pompous lawyer.'

'To make the gesture of rejection,' read Jonathan, 'as if saying "Heaven forfend", the rhetor should push his hands to the left and turn his gaze in the opposite direction.'

Here Lupus pushed his arms straight out to the left, palms forward, and twisted his head and torso as far as he could to the right, a look of extreme repulsion on his face.

Flavia giggled.

'The gesture of amazement is shown by turning the palm slightly upward and closing the fingers one by one, the little finger first, and then opening them up in the reverse order.'

Lupus adopted an amazed look as he watched his own hand make the gesture.

Flavia laughed.

'To express surprise or indignation, DO NOT toss the head and shake the hair about.'

Lupus shook his head wildly so that his hair flopped from one side to the other, then over his eyes.

Flavia was now laughing so hard that she had to sit on the bed beside Jonathan.

'In the face,' continued Jonathan, 'the eyes are most expressive. The rhetor must not abuse their power. His eyes may be intent . . . proud . . . fierce . . . gentle . . . or harsh.'

Lupus imitated each of these expressions in turn, and Flavia laughed at each one.

'*But he must NEVER let his eyes be fixed*' – here Lupus stared at the wall without blinking – '*or popping out*' – Lupus made his bug-eyed look – '*or shifty*' – Lupus narrowed his eyes and without moving his head looked to his extreme left and then right – '*or swimming . . . sleepy . . . stupefied . . . voluptuous . . . or sexy!*'

Lupus demonstrated this last word by wiggling his eyebrows up and down. Flavia and Jonathan both doubled over laughing.

'What are you doing in here?' came a deep voice from the doorway.

'Floppy!' cried Flavia, then clapped her hand over her mouth and burst out laughing again.

Flaccus scowled at her and strode over to the bed. 'That's my Quintilian!' he growled, and snatched up the scroll.

This sent Jonathan into fresh paroxysms of laughter. He tried to speak but was laughing too hard. Finally he managed to point at Flaccus and blurt out: 'It's his . . . Quintilian!'

They collapsed in helpless gales of laughter.

'It's no laughing matter,' said Flaccus, the tips of his ears turning pink. 'It's very serious.'

Over in his corner, Lupus put his hands on his togaed hips and made the expression for 'serious' by pursing his lips, staring with his eyes and thrusting his head forward.

Tears of laughter were now running down Flavia's cheeks and Jonathan was rolling on the bed.

Flaccus snorted, swivelled on his heel and stalked out of the room.

Flavia sent the boys home via the secret passage in her bedroom wall. When she went back to the guest room she found Lynceus quietly folding his master's toga.

'*Abiit, excessit, evasit, erupit,*' said the old slave without looking up. 'He has left, absconded, escaped and disappeared. To quote Cicero.'

'Oh dear,' said Flavia, and went downstairs to look for Flaccus.

He was sitting at the cedarwood table in her father's tablinum, but with his back to the garden. The sun had disappeared behind the city walls and although it was still a few hours until dusk, the air had already grown chilly. She went into the kitchen and returned a few moments later with a cup of hot spiced wine.

'Gaius?' She paused in the tablinum doorway. 'Gaius, I'm sorry.'

Flaccus did not reply. She tipped her head to one side and studied his back. It was a very attractive back: broad and muscular, and at that moment very stiff.

She went to the desk and stood beside him. 'I made you some spiced wine,' she said, 'to warm you up.'

He did not respond or look at her.

'It's well watered.'

Silence.

She sighed and put the cup on the desk beside him. Then she moved closer and looked over his shoulder. A papyrus scroll like the one Jonathan had been reading lay on the desk before him. Beside him was an open tablet. He turned his head to make a note on the red wax and then looked back at the scroll.

'What are you reading?' she asked. Standing this close to him she could feel the warmth radiating from his body and she could smell his distinctive scent: cinnamon and musk.

He put down the ivory stylus and sighed and stared straight ahead.

'I promise I won't laugh,' she said.

'Quintilian,' he said at last. 'I'm reading Quintilian.'

Flavia was glad she was standing behind him. He could not see her biting her lip to keep from giggling.

Presently she managed, 'What's a Quintilian?'

'Not what. Who. Quintilian is the greatest rhetor who ever lived. After Cicero, of course. One day I hope to study with him up in Rome.'

Flavia pulled her father's old leather and oak armchair round to where she could see Flaccus's face. 'Then he's still alive? Quintilian, I mean.'

'Of course he's still alive. He's not yet fifty.'

Flavia sat in the chair and frowned. 'But Cicero's not, is he? He's not alive.'

Flaccus looked up from his scroll and raised an eyebrow.

'Of course Cicero's not alive,' said Flavia quickly. 'He . . . um . . . he lived in the time of the Republic. Julius Caesar. Marcus Antonius. All those people.'

'Yes,' said Flaccus, and returned to his scroll.

'Oh!' said Flavia suddenly. 'Was Cicero the one who had his head and hands cut off and Marcus Antonius's wife took his severed head in her lap and stabbed his lifeless tongue again and again with her hairpin?'

'That's the man,' said Flaccus.

'Nasty end,' murmured Flavia.

'No,' said Flaccus, looking up at her earnestly. 'It was a noble end. Even splendid. He was on his way here to his seaside estate when his enemies caught up with him.

He stuck his head out of the litter, exposed his bare neck and calmly demanded that they do it quickly and well.'

'How brave,' whispered Flavia.

Flaccus nodded. 'Once, when I was studying rhetoric, our master set us a question to debate: *Imagine you are Cicero. Should you beg Marcus Antonius to pardon you? And if Antonius were to agree, but only on the condition that you destroy all your writings, should you accept?*'

'What do you think?'

'If there is any immortality to be had in this world,' said Flaccus quietly, 'it is through the things we write. Cicero made the right decision.' He paused and looked up at her with his dark eyes. 'You know, the anniversary of his death is the day after tomorrow.'

'The day of the trial!' breathed Flavia. 'Do you think it's an omen?'

'I hope not,' he said with a shrug, but she thought she saw him shiver.

'Drink your wine while it's hot,' she said. 'It will warm you.'

He dutifully took a sip from the steaming beaker.

A breeze from the garden brought a scent of winter jasmine and ruffled his glossy dark hair.

Flavia tucked her feet under her and studied him. She always forgot how handsome he was, with his long, thick eyelashes and straight nose and sensitive mouth. She remembered that once she had imagined kissing those lips.

He looked up at her and she felt her cheeks grow warm.

'Flavia,' he said. 'May I tell you something?'

'Of course,' she said brightly.

'Something very personal?'

'Yes.' Her heart beat faster.

'You won't laugh?'

'I promise.'

He looked down at the scroll. 'I'm terrified.'

'Terrified? Of what?'

'Of the trial.' His voice was very low.

'But why?'

'I've never pleaded a case before.'

'But you studied rhetoric, didn't you?'

'Yes. At the academy in Athens.'

'And didn't you say you were going to practise law in Rome?'

'I've been so busy searching for a master criminal that I haven't had a chance.'

'Oh. But didn't you plead cases when you were studying in Athens?'

'Only practice cases, like the one about Cicero. This is real. Someone's freedom is at stake. Maybe their life.' He suddenly seemed very young and vulnerable, and she remembered he was not yet twenty.

'Oh, Gaius!' The leather armchair creaked as she sat forward. 'You'll be marvellous. You have the most marvellous voice, and you look marvellous in a toga and you know lots of Greek and . . . you'll be marvellous!' She felt herself flushing and wondered if she had gone too far.

'You repeated the word *marvellous* too many times,' he said.

But then he smiled at her, and she knew she had said exactly the right thing.

*

'Great Neptune's beard, man!' bellowed a voice from the doorway. 'What are you doing up here in my daughter's bedroom?'

'Pater!' Flavia leapt off the bed and ran to her father and hugged him. 'You're home from Sicily!'

'And not a moment too soon, it seems!'

'Oh, pater! It's only Floppy. He was practising his exordium.'

Marcus Flavius Geminus narrowed his eyes at the young man standing red-faced in the corner of Flavia's bedroom. 'Gaius Valerius Flaccus? Is that you?'

'Hello, sir,' said Flaccus. 'I realise that it's inappropriate for me to be in your daughter's room, but it does have the best mirror. The great Demosthenes used to practise in front of a full-length mirror,' he added.

'Gaius is practising the gestures,' said Flavia. 'Apparently, good rhetors have to know all the gestures.'

Flaccus nodded. 'Gestures plus voice equal delivery, and delivery is the most important element of great oratory. As Demosthenes himself said: *Delivery, delivery, and delivery.*'

Flavia saw her father suppress a smile. 'Gestures and oratory are all well and good, Valerius Flaccus, but not in my daughter's bedroom. Come. Let's go downstairs. Alma has just put a patina in the oven and I can already smell it. I'm famished.'

Flavia's father stepped aside to let Flaccus pass, then turned to give her his sternest paterfamilias expression.

'Pater!' she cried, before he could rebuke her. 'Nubia almost witnessed a murder! But she's still officially your slave and so they could torture her. She's had to flee to Uncle Gaius's farm. You can't have dinner until you've gone and set her free.'

By the time they finally sat down to dinner, it was after dusk and Caudex was already lighting the hanging oil-lamps. Their main course was soup, so the adults joined Flavia and Nubia at the table. Scuto and Nipur crowded happily underneath, jostling knees in the hope of morsels.

'Oh, Nubia,' said Flavia, giving her friend a hug. 'It's so good to have you home. I missed you.'

'I missed you, too,' said Nubia. 'But Gaius and Miriam are very kind. They feed me and hide me in wine press.' She slipped Nipur a secret piece of flat-bread.

Flavia's father blew on a spoonful of pea and leek soup. 'Yes, you were lucky not to be discovered. Another bit of good luck was meeting that decurion on his way back from young Pliny's estate. He witnessed Nubia's manumission right there on the Laurentum Road. Here it is.' He tapped a wax tablet on the table beside him. 'All signed and sealed. I'll pay your slave-tax first thing tomorrow. But now that I'm back, I don't think they'll try such low tricks again. Who do you think was behind Nubia's arrest, anyway?'

'It had to be someone,' said Aristo, 'who knows us well enough to have realised that Nubia's original manumission wasn't strictly legal.'

'Or someone who has access to someone who knows you that well,' said Flaccus.

'Or it could be someone who knows how Nubia was set free last year at the Villa of Pollius Felix,' murmured Flavia. Suddenly she had a terrible thought and looked up to find Flaccus looking back at her. She knew he was thinking the same thing, because she could see the muscles of his jaw clenching. 'You don't think it could be Felix?' she whispered.

Flavia's father looked at her with interest. 'Why would Pollius Felix want to hurt us?'

'No reason,' said Flavia hastily.

To her relief, Flaccus said, 'I think we need to search closer to home.' He turned to Aristo. 'Flavia tells me you've been trying to find out more about Dives. Any luck? At the moment I have precious little to build a case on.'

'I've learned that Dives was not always rich,' said Aristo. 'He was born a plebeian: Gaius Artorius Brutus was the name he used to go by. His father was a poor farmer from Paestum and his mother a Greek freedwoman. He joined the army, served with the Tenth Legion in Judaea. He was wounded ten years ago, during the siege of Jerusalem. He stayed in the army for a few more years, then was granted early discharge. He came back to Italia, bought the estate near Laurentum and lived there for almost five years, growing richer and richer, fatter and fatter. At some point he changed his cognomen from Brutus to Dives.' Aristo dipped a hunk of rye bread into his soup.

Flavia's father frowned. 'How was it,' he said, 'that a retired legionary was able to buy a seaside estate at Laurentum, with olive groves, vineyards, mulberry orchards and a thousand head of cattle?'

'Yes,' said Flaccus. 'How did Gaius Artorius Brutus become Gaius Artorius Dives?'

'There are several theories,' said Aristo, 'the most likely being that he stumbled across some jewel or treasure when serving in Judaea and when he returned to Italia he sold this and made his fortune.'

'It must have been a big jewel,' said Flavia.

'Indeed.' Aristo mopped the bottom of his soup bowl with his bread. 'They say his estate was worth two million sesterces when he bought it. Now it is worth ten times that.'

'Could he have inherited the money?' asked Flaccus.

'Dives did inherit his father's farm in Calabria,' said Aristo. 'But it was small and barren. He sold it for a pittance and ploughed the money into his Laurentum estate.'

'What about the man himself?' asked Flaccus. 'What did people think of Dives?'

'His slaves considered him to be a good master,' said Aristo. 'And by the way, most of them are Jews. But he wasn't well-respected by the neighbouring landowners or by people of the upper class.'

'Why not?' said Flaccus, making notes on his red wax tablet. Flavia noticed he had barely touched his soup.

'Dives welcomed the attention of legacy-hunters. That's not considered proper behaviour among men of your class, is it?'

'Certainly not,' said Flaccus.

Aristo nodded. 'Well, apparently he encouraged them to bring him pastries, and read him the latest poetry from Rome, and accompany him on foot when he was carried in his sedan chair. The usual things.'

'Why?' said Nubia. 'Why do people bring him pastry and read poetry?'

'Dives was fabulously wealthy,' said Aristo with a smile. 'But he had no obvious heirs. Some people hoped that if they were especially kind to him when he was alive, then he would leave them money after his death.'

'And he encouraged these captators?' asked Flaccus.

'He did indeed. He loved the attention. Although everyone suspected he would make young Nonius his heir, they lived in hope of juicy legacies. Indeed, he often made a great show of bringing out his will in order to add a codicil or rub something out. He made a lot of enemies when he died.'

'Why?' asked Flavia's father.

'He only left his captators five sesterces each,' said Aristo. 'Some of the citizens I spoke to approved, but others thought his behaviour despicable.'

'*Could* he have been murdered?' asked Flaccus. 'Nonius has accused my client of murdering Dives.'

Flavia put down her spoon. 'Didn't I tell you what Jonathan discovered?' she asked.

'No,' they all said.

'There's a rumour that Dives was smothered. According to a Jewish freedwoman who lives on the estate.'

'Why hasn't she told the authorities about this?' asked Marcus.

'The rumour started with the slaves,' said Flavia.

'And as we now know,' said Aristo, with a nod towards Nubia, 'the testimony of a slave is not valid unless they have been tortured.'

'So none of them will go running to the authorities,' said Flaccus drily.

'And the freedwoman won't tell because she probably doesn't want to see her friends hurt,' added Flavia. 'According to Jonathan she was a slave, too, until last week.'

'Dives freed her in his will?' said Flaccus.

'I think so,' said Flavia.

Flaccus took out his red wax tablet. 'What's this freedwoman's name?' he asked.

'I can't remember. Jonathan will know.'

Flaccus closed his tablet. 'I'll ask him tomorrow.'

Flavia's father gave Flaccus a keen glance. 'You've hardly touched your soup,' he said. 'Nervous?'

Flaccus glanced at Flavia and she gave him an encouraging smile.

'Terrified,' said Flaccus. 'I don't suppose *you'd* like to defend Hephzibah the day after tomorrow?'

'I'm afraid I can't,' said Marcus. 'I'm due to attend a ceremony at my patron's house that day. And I'm busy all day tomorrow. I'm supervising the redecoration of Cordius' bedroom before he and his bride return.'

'Pater!' cried Flavia. 'Aren't you even coming to the trial?'

Marcus shook his head. 'I'm sorry. Cordius is making a new will the day after tomorrow, and I've promised to be a witness. I think he wants to leave his estate to his new wife.'

'But he just married her,' said Flavia. 'Won't she automatically inherit?'

'Not at all,' said her father. 'According to Roman law, wives and husbands have no automatic claim on each other's property. If she's not named in his will then the estate could be bitterly contested after his death. And Cordius has plenty of legacy-hunters eager to do such a thing. They won't be pleased about the new will, but it might thin them out. I'll be glad to see the back of them.'

'Cordius has legacy-hunters?' asked Flavia. 'I didn't know that.'

'Of course he has legacy-hunters,' said her father.

'Until he got married last week he was the perfect type of fish for them to cast their baited lines to: childless, rich and old.'

'Childless, rich and old,' echoed Flaccus, and glanced over his shoulder at Lynceus, who stood quietly behind him. Flavia saw Lynceus give his young master a sad nod. Flaccus turned back. 'I hate legacy-hunters. They cultivated my father even though he wasn't childless. But I was his only obvious heir, and I always felt them watching me and hoping for me to die first.'

'I wonder if Nonius was a captator,' mused Flavia.

'I forget which one is Nonius,' said Nubia. 'Their names are most confusing.'

'Nonius is the man who inherited Dives's estate,' explained Flavia. 'The man with the light brown skin and swollen eye. He's the one who's accusing Hephzibah of murder.'

Aristo shrugged. 'Some say Nonius was a captator, and some say no. But Nonius's father was Dives's best friend and tentmate when they served together in Judaea. So I'm guessing he was a genuine friend rather than an inheritance-hunter.'

Flaccus shook his head. 'I wonder if any rich man has true friends. There's a saying doing the rounds of Rome at the moment: *If you're childless, rich and getting old, your so-called friends are probably after your gold.*'

The sixth day of December dawned clear and cold. The four friends spent the whole morning lesson studying the basics of rhetoric, on Flavia's request. She wanted to be able to understand the next day's court case, and Aristo agreed this was a useful thing to know.

The winter sun had almost reached its zenith when a

knock came at the front door. Caudex was out shopping with Alma so Lupus ran forward to push back the bolt and open the door.

It was Flaccus and his slave. 'Sorry to interrupt your lesson.' Flaccus was unwrapping his toga as he walked across the atrium towards the inner garden. 'We've spent the whole morning interviewing Hephzibah of Jerusalem, one of the seven survivors of Masada. I have a few more witnesses to interview before I write my speech. I'll leave you to finish your lesson.'

'No!' cried Flavia. 'Don't go! We've been studying the six parts of a speech all morning. Test us!'

Flaccus paused in the corridor leading into the inner garden and turned back to them with a smile. 'Very quickly, then,' he said to them. He handed his toga to Lynceus. 'Take this up to my room and bring down my travelling cloak.'

'Yes, master,' said Lynceus, and left.

Flaccus turned back to them. 'Go on, then, Flavia,' he said with a smile. 'Tell me the first part of a speech.'

'The prologue!' cried Flavia. 'The beginning of your speech is the prologue.'

Flaccus nodded. 'Very good! I call it the exordium, as Quintilian does. This is when I must gain the sympathy of the judges and spectators.' He winked at Aristo, who was sitting back in his chair with his arms folded across his chest. 'Did your tutor teach you the next step?'

'Yes!' cried Flavia. 'The narration. Where you tell what happened. Like a story.'

Aristo gave a grunt of approval.

'And after the narration?' said Flaccus. 'What comes next? Somebody other than Flavia?'

Jonathan looked up at the ceiling. 'The proposition,'

he recited, 'in which you present your case and the line of argument you intend to take.'

'Exactly so. And then we have . . . Lupus?'

Lupus held up his wax tablet. On it he had written the six steps of a rhetor's speech. He pointed to the fourth item on the list: PROOFS.

Flaccus leaned forward, squinted at the tablet, then added. 'Correct. Proofs are next, when you back up your theory with facts, witnesses and evidence.'

'Then comes the refutation,' said Flavia, 'where you try to guess which arguments your opponent might have and refute them before he can even list them.'

'Excellent,' said Flaccus. 'Nubia. Can you tell me the final and sixth step of the orator's speech?'

Nubia gazed up at him and solemnly shook her head. 'All the words are sounding the same to me,' she said.

Flaccus smiled. 'The final part of the rhetor's speech is called the peroration. That is when I must sum up the case, appeal to the judges' better nature and ask them to vote justly.'

'It is very confusing,' said Nubia in a small voice.

Lupus tapped her shoulder and held up his wax tablet.

They all looked at Lupus's tablet. On it he had added explanations for each of the six steps.

EXORDIUM	INTRODUCTION
NARRATION	WHAT HAPPENED BEFORE THE CRIME
PROPOSITION	HOW THE CRIME WAS COMMITTED
PROOFS	EVIDENCE AND CLUES

| REFUTATION | HOW YOUR OPPONENT IS WRONG |
| PERORATION | CONCLUSION |

Nubia's amber eyes lit up. 'Oh! I understand,' she said. 'Thank you, Lupus.'

'Well done, Lupus,' said Aristo. 'You've put the six parts of an orator's speech in terms that are clear and simple.'

Flaccus sighed. 'I just hope I can state the case as clearly tomorrow.'

'Oh, Lupus,' said Flavia, 'if only you could speak, you'd be a brilliant orator.'

'He doesn't need to speak,' said Flaccus. 'Don't you know the story of the King of Pontus and the pantomimes?'

'What is pant oh mine?' asked Nubia.

Aristo smiled. 'It's a type of play in which the lead actor wears a mask and acts out a story with dance and gestures. He is accompanied by a chorus singing the story, and by musical instruments.'

'And the lead actor is called a pantomime, too,' said Flaccus, turning to go to his room.

'Don't go yet, Floppy!' cried Flavia. 'Tell us the story about the king and the pantomimes!'

Flaccus shook his head. 'I've got to ride out to Laurentum,' he said, 'and make some enquiries.'

'Oh, please tell us! Just the short version.'

He sighed and turned back to them. 'Very well; the short version. It happened in the time of Nero, when my father was a senator. The King of Pontus was visiting Rome and Nero took him to see some panto-mimes. Having no Latin, the King of Pontus couldn't understand the words of the songs or speeches, but the gestures of the pantomimes were so clear that he was able to follow the performances from beginning to end. The king begged Nero to give him some of the panto-mimes, saying he could take them home and use them instead of interpreters. Of course we orators do not like to be grouped with pantomimes, but the principle is the same. You can speak very eloquently through gesture.'

Lupus spread his hands, as if to say *There you are*, and when they all laughed he bowed.

Lynceus appeared from the direction of the inner garden. He held his master's travelling cloak in his hands.

'*Tempus fugit!*' he said, 'Time flies.'

'Well put,' said Flaccus and accepted the cloak. 'We've got to fly, too.'

'Where are you going?' asked Flavia.

'We're going to Nonius's estate. I want to talk to . . .' He glanced at Jonathan.

'Restituta,' said Jonathan.

'Restituta,' said Flaccus, 'to get to the bottom of the rumour that Dives was murdered. I also want to inter-view the slaves and freedmen, too. I hope to find out more about Dives and Nonius, their former and present masters.'

'Then you're not going to the synagogue?'

He frowned. 'Why would I go to the synagogue?'

Without answering him Flavia excitedly turned to Aristo. 'Please, may we go to the synagogue?' she asked. 'I think I've just realised what *find the other six* means!'

'That boy and his family follow a blasphemous doc-trine,' said the rabbi gruffly, glowering down at

Jonathan. He turned to Flavia, 'But you and he have been doing good deeds in the community. For that reason I will grant you a short interview.'

'Thank you, sir,' said Flavia politely. She and her friends followed the bearded, turbaned Jew through the arched doorway of the synagogue. As they emerged into the bright inner courtyard, Flavia looked around.

Two summers ago, she and Jonathan and Nubia had come here to hide from kidnappers. The fig tree was bare now, but it was a sunny morning and the rabbi indicated that they should sit on a marble bench beneath it. He clapped his hands and a few moments later a boy in a cream tunic brought out a light table with steaming beakers of sweet sage tea and almond pastries. The boy put the table before the bench and disappeared back inside.

'Tell me,' said the rabbi. 'How can I help you.'

'Have you heard of the case of Hephzibah of Jerusalem?' asked Flavia.

The rabbi nodded. 'Yes, I have heard. Some of the freedmen from Nonius's estate attend our services. Again I say: it is a good deed you are doing, defending her.'

'Did you know that she was one of the seven survivors of Masada?' asked Jonathan.

The rabbi nodded solemnly. 'I know.'

'We think,' said Flavia, 'that the other survivors might provide a clue to the death of the magistrate Papillio. His dying words were *find the other six*. we know that Hephzibah's mother died last year, so now there are only five. Do you know where any of them are?'

'I only know where one of them is,' said the rabbi. 'A

youth called Zechariah. He was the youngest of them and he is now nine years old.'

'Zechariah!' cried Flavia, and looked excitedly at the others. 'I think that was the name of the little boy who got hungry.' She turned back to the rabbi. 'Can you tell us where he is?'

'I can do better than that,' said the rabbi. He clapped his hands again and the serving-boy reappeared. 'Zechariah,' said the rabbi, 'these children are friends of one of your fellow-survivors. They would like to speak to you.'

'Did you learn anything useful at the synagogue?' Flaccus asked Flavia later that afternoon as they ate an early dinner of hot bean soup and cold roast chicken.

Flavia put down her spoon and shook her head. 'Not really,' she said, 'but we met the youngest survivor of Masada, a boy named Zechariah. He was taken to Rome along with the others. Do you know Josephus? The Emperor's freedman, who's writing about the Jewish Wars?'

'I've heard of him,' said Flaccus, 'but I've never met him.'

'Well, Josephus bought all seven survivors, but eventually he sold Zechariah and the other three children to a tavern-owner in Rome. They died in the fever last year, all apart from Zechariah. He was the only one to survive. He's nine years old now. The priest from the synagogue bought him and has adopted him.'

'Rabbi,' said Jonathan, mopping his empty bowl with a piece of bread. 'The priest is called a rabbi.'

'What about the old woman?' asked Flaccus, taking a piece of chicken from the platter. 'Hephzibah told me there was an old woman who survived the siege, too.'

'Yes, but according to Zechariah she died while they were still in the service of Josephus.'

'So those weren't the six you're looking for?'

'No,' sighed Flavia. 'It was an empty amphora. How about you? Did you visit Nonius's estate?'

'Yes,' said Flaccus, 'Luckily Nonius wasn't there; I don't think he would have been very welcoming. But his bailiff was. He took me to interview Restituta and some of the slaves.'

'What did Artoria Restituta say?' asked Flavia.

'Not much. As you guessed, she is reluctant to say which of the slaves claims that Dives was smothered. If she named him, he would be arrested and tortured. I also saw Hephzibah's friend, Priscilla.'

'Slave-girl who is pregnant,' said Nubia.

'Yes.'

'What did she say?' asked Flavia.

'Nothing, really. She just said that everybody loved Hephzibah, especially the children on the estate.' Flaccus tossed a chicken bone onto the floor. 'Oh, she did say one curious thing.'

'Yes?' They all looked at him.

'She said she couldn't wait to live with Hephzibah.'

'What does that mean?'

'I don't know. When I asked her she suddenly sank to a chair and claimed to feel weak. She's terribly young – not much older than you two girls – and terribly pregnant. I'm not an expert on these things, but I'd say she's overdue.'

'And did you learn anything from your interview with Hephzibah this morning?' asked Aristo.

Flaccus shook his head. 'Nothing new. Nothing you hadn't told us before. Poor girl. She reminds me of Cassandra, the red-haired princess who survived the terrible destruction of Troy only to find death in the land of her captors.'

'Did Cassandra have red hair?' murmured Flavia. 'I didn't know that.'

'I feel like Cassandra,' said Jonathan. 'I keep having these dreams and nobody believes me.'

'*Ora non umquam credita*,' said a voice. 'Lips that are never believed.' They all looked up to see Lynceus standing in the doorway. 'Virgil,' he said, and added. 'It will be dark soon, master, and you have a long day tomorrow.'

'You're like an old nursemaid,' grumbled Flaccus. 'But you're right. I have a big day tomorrow and I should retire. I want to get up before dawn to make a sacrifice to Janus, the god of good beginnings.'

On the morning of the trial, Jonathan woke in a cold sweat, his heart pounding and his mind spinning. He had dreamt the dream again. The dream about the funeral on the foggy day. It had seemed so real. He could still smell the fog, and the myrrh used to anoint corpses.

He sat up too quickly and felt sick. He waited for the nausea to pass, then wondered whether to lie down again or go to the latrine.

'I'm going to die,' he whispered. 'Or someone close to me. Dear Lord, please avert this disaster.'

There was a grunt to his left. Jonathan turned to see Lupus, sitting on his bed. Lupus looked as pale as Jonathan felt.

'What? What is it, Lupus?'

His friend held out a wax tablet.

It was not sealed, so Jonathan opened it.

A moment later he looked up at Lupus. 'Master of the Universe, Lupus! What possessed you to write this today? It's your last will and testament.'

LAST WILL AND TESTAMENT OF LUPUS.

I LEAVE MY SHIP, THE DELPHINA, TO MY FRIEND JONATHAN BEN MORDECAI, WHO TOOK ME INTO HIS HOME AND LET ME SHARE HIS BEDROOM.

I ASK THAT MY GOLD BE DIVIDED FOUR WAYS. ONE PART TO JONATHAN, ONE PART TO FLAVIA GEMINA AND ONE PART TO NUBIA. THE REMAINING QUARTER IS TO BE SENT TO MY MOTHER, WHO SERVES THE GOD APOLLO AT DELPHI. I ALSO ASK THAT JONATHAN, FLAVIA AND NUBIA WILL BE KIND TO HER AND CARE FOR HER AS IF SHE WERE THEIR OWN MOTHER.

HERE ENDS THE WILL OF LUPUS, WRITTEN THIS SEVENTH DAY BEFORE THE IDES OF DECEMBER IN THE SECOND YEAR OF TITUS.

SCROLL XII

It was a mild winter morning. A pearly skin of high cloud covered the domed sky, like the membrane on a boiled egg.

In the middle of the forum, Praeco the town crier stood on his plinth, announcing the trial and summoning various witnesses and citizens. The ground floor of Ostia's basilica was already crowded with people when Aristo and the four friends arrived.

Flavia had visited the offices on the first floor but she had never been on the vast ground floor of the basilica itself. Its lofty central nave was flanked by elegant columns of polished marble: pink veined with grey. The floor was made of highly polished marble, too: squares of inlaid apricot on creamy white.

'Behold!' cried Nubia, looking up. 'Pigeons.'

Flavia tipped her head back as she followed Nubia's gaze up the polished columns to the distant roof. Pigeons fluttered high above them, dots against the high painted ceiling. Arched windows let in the pearly light of the bright December morning.

'Great Juno's peacock,' she cried. 'It's huge.'

'It makes for a dramatic sense of space and light,' shouted Aristo over the babble of the crowd, 'but the acoustics are dire. Particularly when you have more than one case in progress.'

Flavia looked at him in surprise. 'They have more than one case at a time in here?'

He nodded. 'Sometimes as many as four at a time. They screen them off with curtains. My friend Leander and I occasionally come to watch from the gallery. Especially if someone famous is pleading. Luckily ours is the only case today.'

'All these people come to see Hephzibah?' asked Nubia.

Aristo nodded. 'This is the first murder trial they've had here in years; most murder cases are tried up in Rome.'

'Great Juno's peacock!' muttered Flavia, as a man jostled her. 'It's getting too crowded in here.'

'Come this way,' said Aristo, linking his right arm through Flavia's and his left through Nubia's.

At the southern end of the basilica was an empty square area marked off by scarlet ropes and marble benches. Behind a rank of tiered marble benches at the basilica's far end stood a large cube of white marble with a bronze chair on top.

'What is that?' said Nubia, pointing.

'That's the podium, or dais,' said Aristo. 'It's where the chairman for the most important hearing sits. Today, that's us.' He pointed. 'Those tiered seats below the podium are for the judges. Probably thirty decurions for this case. The benches to the chairman's left are for the prosecutors and the ones on his right for the defence. And the ones on the end are for witnesses and distinguished guests. Do you see how the four ranks of benches form a small courtyard? That's where the lawyers stand to plead their case. Speaking of the lawyer, here he is now.'

Flavia saw Flaccus's slave Lynceus clearing a way through the crowd. Behind him came Flaccus in a red-bordered toga, flanked by two women whose pallas covered their heads and lower faces. Hephzibah wore black and the woman beside her wore dark blue.

'Who's that with Hephzibah?' said Flavia with a frown. 'Is it Jonathan's mother?'

'Yes,' said Nubia. 'I think it is Susannah.'

Behind the two women came Jonathan and Lupus, both wearing their best tunics and togas. Flavia and Nubia waved to them. Flaccus said something to the boys, who pushed through the crowd and ran up to them.

'Where's Miriam,' Flavia asked Jonathan, 'and your father? I thought they were coming.'

'Father had to see a patient on the other side of town,' said Jonathan, 'and Miriam's attending a child-birth up at Nonius's estate. That slave-girl: Priscilla. They'll both be here as soon as they can. Flaccus wants us to sit on the defence benches,' he added, wheezing a little with excitement.

'Oh, good! I thought we'd have to watch from up there.' Flavia glanced up at the faces looking back down at her from the upper gallery.

'I'm guessing he wants as many supporters as possible sitting with him,' said Aristo, lifting the scarlet cord so they could pass through to the marble benches. 'There aren't as many of us as there are of them.'

'You can say that again!' Flavia looked towards the benches opposite, where togaed men were taking their seats. 'I don't think they'll all fit.'

Aristo frowned. 'It looks as if they have at least three lawyers for the prosecution and about a dozen assistants.'

'Good morning, Flaccus!' said Flavia brightly, as Flaccus and Lynceus came up to them. 'Good morning, Hephzibah,' and to Jonathan's mother: 'Good morning, domina.'

'Good morning,' Flaccus replied and they all greeted one another.

Flavia smiled up at Flaccus and said shyly, 'You look marvellous.'

'*Vestis virum reddit*,' said Lynceus. 'Clothes make the man. Quintilian himself says that.'

Flaccus nodded and gestured for Flavia and her friends to sit on the bench behind the first one, where he would sit beside Hephzibah and Susannah.

When they were all seated, Flavia leaned forward and patted Flaccus on the back, 'Good luck!' she said brightly.

He gave her a queasy smile over his shoulder.

Opposite them, the lawyers for the prosecution were taking their seats, too. Suddenly Lupus grunted and pointed.

'Behold!' said Nubia. 'One of the lawyers is Bato.'

'You're right!' exclaimed Flavia. 'It's Marcus Artorius Bato.'

'The man who sailed with us to Rhodes last spring?' said Flaccus. 'And who helped us rescue the kidnapped children?' He was nearsighted and had to narrow his eyes to see.

'Yes,' said Flavia. 'I wonder why he's on their side?'

'They paid him a cartload of silver?' suggested Jonathan.

'Lawyers don't get paid,' said Aristo. 'They do it as a public service and to climb the ladder of honours.'

'They do not receive money?' said Nubia.

'Well, not officially. I'm sure some receive gifts from grateful clients.' Aristo leaned towards Flaccus and lowered his voice. 'The thin one examining the sheet of papyrus is Lucius Cartilius Poplicola, a member of one of Ostia's most eminent families. He's supposed to be ruthless.'

'Who's the handsome one?' said Flavia. 'The big one with dark hair and blue eyes. I've never seen him before.'

'Dear gods, no,' said Flaccus, squinting.

'What?' Flavia looked at him, alarmed.

'By Hercules!' said Aristo. 'Is that who I think it is?'

Flaccus nodded. His back was rigid.

Lynceus opened his mouth, then closed it again. He obviously had no motto for this situation.

'Who is it?' cried Flavia. 'Who?'

'It's Quintilian,' said Aristo.

'*The* Quintilian?' said Jonathan.

Aristo nodded grimly: 'The *the* himself.'

The judges had taken their places and for a moment the buzzing subsided as a fat bald man in a toga mounted the podium. 'That's the chairman,' said Aristo. 'Titus Hostilius Gratus. He's a duovir. They say he's a hard man, but fair.'

The main floor and galleries of the basilica were now packed and the echoing din of the crowd was so loud that Flavia and Nubia covered their ears.

Abruptly Praeco appeared. He had put on his best

toga and now he walked importantly up the steps of the podium to take on the role of herald. His bronze staff rang out as he banged it sharply on the marble podium. 'ALL QUIET! ALL QUIET, PLEASE!'

The crowd grew instantly quiet and the chairman – Gratus – stood and covered his bald head with his toga. As he began to invoke the gods, Flavia leaned forward a little in order to study Hephzibah.

The slave-girl sat with straight back and raised chin. Her hair was modestly covered by the black palla of mourning. Although her eyes stared straight ahead, she was not looking at her accuser on the bench opposite. She seemed to be gazing into the past.

Gratus finished reading the charges and cleared his throat: 'I would like to invite first the prosecution and then the defence to present their exordium. You each will have one clepsydra.'

'What is klep seed rah?' whispered Nubia.

'It's that thing made of copper and glass, on the table beside the judge's podium,' said Flavia.

'It's a water clock,' said Jonathan. 'It measures time according to the flow of water.'

'A clepsydra is also a unit of time,' said Aristo. 'There are about three in an hour.'

'Then,' continued bald Gratus, 'we shall hear the evidence, with three clepsydras allotted to each side.' He turned to Nonius's side of the court. 'The prosecution may begin.'

Praeco stood and banged his bronze staff on the marble podium. 'THIS COURT,' he blasted, 'IS NOW IN SESSION! MARCUS FABIUS QUINTILIANUS TO SPEAK FOR THE PROSECUTION!'

*

As the renowned Quintilian rose to his feet, a murmur of excitement washed over the spectators, then receded with a sigh, like a wave on sand. Everyone wanted to hear Rome's greatest living orator.

He was a big man, solid rather than fat, and light on his feet. Flavia guessed he was in his mid-forties. His dark hair was lightly oiled and his toga perfectly draped. He slowly swivelled on one foot, sweeping the spectators with a gaze as blue and sharp as an icicle.

For a moment he closed his eyes, as if to savour the silence. Then he spoke.

'Esteemed chairman and judges,' he began in a clear voice. 'We are gathered here today on a most extraordinary and sad occasion. A terrible crime has occurred here in Ostia, the great port of Rome. The crime, a triple-homicide, is something unheard of in my experience. Because the accused is a slave – or at any rate of questionable status – the case could not be heard in Rome.

'I must confess that I was so intrigued by this case, that I decided to come down from my Sabine vineyards and participate.' Quintilian's voice was soft, and yet Flavia could see by the happily attentive faces of those high above her that it carried all the way to the galleries.

'I have studied the briefs,' he continued, 'and I would like to give a simple overview of the case, as much for my understanding of the matter as for yours.'

Quintilian gestured elegantly towards Hephzibah, sitting rigid and remote on her bench. 'This girl, Hephzibah bat David, of Jerusalem, was sold along with her mother at an auction of slaves in Rome, at about this time last year. The ex-legionary-turned-land-owner Gaius Artorius Dives purchased the two women himself. We have the document here.' He accepted a wax tablet from one of his assistants, flipped it open and nodded. 'The purchase agreement states that Hephzibah and her mother Rachel were both skilled seamstresses and weavers. The price paid for the two was four thousand sesterces; that is two thousand each. The purchase document is sealed with Dives's signet-ring, which bears the imprint of Hercules in a lionskin wielding his club.'

Quintilian handed the tablet to a court official, who put it on a small table in front of the judges.

'Within a month,' said Quintilian, 'the girl's mother was dead. Struck down by the fever which ravaged Rome and Ostia last winter; a fever which made no distinction between class or wealth.'

'By Apollo, he's good!' murmured Aristo. 'The odour of justice hangs about him like the scent of an expensive perfume.'

'The girl was now alone,' said Quintilian, 'and free from parental supervision. Perhaps because of this, we believe she set her sights on nothing less than becoming the wife of Dives. Slaves and freedmen from his estate claim that after her mother's death, she spent more and more time with him. Alone.'

On the bench in front of them, Flavia saw Flaccus lean over and ask Hephzibah a question. She nodded and turned her head to look at him and Flavia caught the words, 'He just liked to talk to me.'

'Then one day, less than a week ago,' continued Quintilian, 'raised voices were heard coming from Dives's bedroom. Shortly afterwards a garden-slave saw Hephzibah running from this same bedroom in tears, screaming *I hate you!* Two days later he was dead.'

Quintilian paused and the whole basilica seemed to hold its breath. Until this moment Quintilian had been in fluid motion, his body turning, his right arm keeping subtle time to the rhythm of his words, his hands perfectly expressing his thoughts. But now – for a long moment – he was perfectly still, and the crowds were still too, as if held by some spell.

As he began to move again, everyone exhaled.

'My colleagues and I believe this is what happened. Hephzibah tried to convince Dives to set her free and marry her. Once she was married and named in his will, she only had to wait for him to die. Then she would be a wealthy woman. But Dives refused her advances. Scorned and shamed, she ran out of his bedroom in tears. Two days later, tormented by grief and rage, she murdered him as he slept.'

The crowd gasped.

'Hephzibah of Jerusalem knew that if her crime should be discovered, her fate would be horrible indeed: crucifixion. So, in desperation, she made up the story that Dives had set her free shortly before he died. No longer a slave and without the ties that bind a freedwoman to her new patron, she could escape with impunity.'

'What does he mean?' whispered Nubia in Flavia's ear.

'If she was free she could run far away.'

With a stately sidelong sweep of his arm, Quintilian turned towards Nonius, glowering on the accuser's bench and sporting a spectacular black eye.

'Hephzibah's new owner, my client, asked the girl for some proof of her new status. A document of manumission. Or at the very least, the name of the witness. It was a reasonable request. But Hephzibah of Jerusalem seemed flustered and confused, saying she did not know where the document was, nor could she remember the man's name. Finally she came up with the name *Gaius Helvidius Pupienus*.'

Quintilian's mouth curved in a faint smile. 'Esteemed judges,' he said, 'there is no such person. However, a certain Ostian magistrate was found, one Gnaeus Helvius Papillio, who did in fact have occasional dealings with Dives. But on the morning of the hearing, the morning when a simple yes or no from Papillio might have proved her claim to Roman citizenship, this unhappy man was stabbed to death.'

Once again a rumble of excited outrage ran round the courtroom.

'The blow was clumsy, I might even say "feeble", as if delivered by someone unused to wielding a sword. And although it took the wretched man a long time to die, that "feeble" blow proved to be deadly. A few hours later, around noon of the very same day,' said Quintilian in his softly compelling voice, 'another man – Mercator – met his death in a most brutal fashion, killed with a single blow to the head in *that girl's cubicle*.' Here Quintilian turned towards Hephzibah in a fluid and dramatic motion. When the excited buzzing of the crowd had once again subsided, Quintilian shook his head sadly.

'Until Mercator's death, nobody suspected this young woman of being a murderess. But after his murder – so clearly at her hand – the facts lead us to the inescapable conclusion that she was also the cause of the first two deaths. In other words, by trying to cover her tracks, she clearly revealed her guilt.'

Quintilian waited for the excited murmur to subside, then fixed the judges with his cool gaze. 'Esteemed Judges,' he said, 'we put our trust in your judgement and integrity. As you hear the evidence to come, I know you will weigh it carefully and I know that in the end, you will make the right decision.'

SCROLL XIII

Now it was Flaccus's turn to introduce his case.

Praeco stood and rapped and bellowed, 'GAIUS VALERIUS FLACCUS TO SPEAK FOR THE DEFENCE!'

Flaccus stood, and Flavia saw his broad back swell as he took a deep breath.

'You can do it, Gaius,' she whispered, and felt her heart thumping hard. 'I know you'll be marvellous.'

Flaccus turned towards the podium and cleared his throat. 'Esteemed Chairman and Judges,' he began. 'You must find it very surprising to see me standing here and addressing you when all these noble orators and distinguished citizens remain seated.'

A ripple of laughter ran through the crowd. Some of the judges snickered and the chairman raised an eyebrow. On the bench in front of them Lynceus stared at his young master in wide-eyed disbelief.

'Oh please, no,' muttered Aristo.

'What is it?' Flavia asked Aristo. 'Why are they laughing?'

'He's quoting Cicero.'

'What's wrong with that?' whispered Flavia. 'Cicero is his idol.'

'Cicero is the idol of every law student.' Aristo gazed up at the lofty ceiling.

'Comparing himself to Cicero is hubris,' said Jonathan. 'Even I know that.'

'Hubris,' said Nubia, 'means overweening pride.'

'That's right,' said Aristo grimly. 'He might as well ask Jupiter to blast him with a bolt of lightning. Dear gods, what is he thinking?'

'I cannot compare myself with these prestigious personages,' Flaccus was saying, 'in either age or influence or experience.' Flaccus touched the tip of his thumb to the tips of his first three fingers and brought his hand to his chest; then allowed his arm to fall down in the gesture of humility.

'No!' whimpered Aristo. 'Not the gestures. Please not the gestures.'

'But a good rhetor has to use the gestures,' said Flavia. 'Quintilian himself says so in scroll eleven. Gestures plus voice equal delivery, and delivery is the most important element of great oratory.'

Flaccus swept his arm from left to right. 'Almost everyone here,' he said, 'is convinced that this girl is guilty.' His toga swirled as he pivoted on one foot and pointed at Hephzibah.

'No, no, no,' moaned Aristo. 'Swinging togas are bad. Bad, bad, bad.'

Flaccus lifted the forefinger of his right hand in the gesture of declamation. 'But I maintain,' he said, 'that she is innocent. Do I imply—' now he was pointing at himself '— that I know something they do not?' He raised his forearm again, and, keeping his elbow stationary he moved his index finger back and forth. 'Not at all. For I am the least knowledgeable of all these. And if I know something—' he tapped the side of his head '— it is not that they do not know, but rather that I know more.'

'What in Hades is he blathering on about?' said Jonathan.

Lynceus's head was in his hands and the crowd was giggling.

'I don't know,' moaned Aristo. 'He should have stuck with Cicero.'

'But you just said it was hubris to quote Cicero,' protested Flavia.

'Better to be struck by lightning than to die slowly and painfully, like Marsyas flayed alive.'

'But I, on the contrary, will point out what needs to be pointed out and say what needs to be said. If I speak wrongly, either nobody will hear of it, for I have not started my public career, or if they do hear of it, they will pardon the error on account of my youthful years.'

Flaccus faced the judges and struck the classic pose of the orator, with one hand raised for silence. 'Why am I defending this girl?' he said. 'On the one hand—'

'Not the hands!' groaned Aristo. 'Please, dear Apollo, deliver us from this torment.'

Flaccus had not quite finished his exordium when the clepsydra chimed and Praeco bellowed: 'TIME!'

Flaccus nodded towards the podium and retreated back to his bench. He was sweating and his face wore a hunted look. Flavia gave him a bright smile of encouragement, but he did not seem to notice. She realised he had said very little about the case itself.

'THE PROSECUTION,' announced Praeco, 'WILL SPEAK AGAIN!'

From the benches opposite, Lucius Cartilius Popli-cola was the next to rise.

Everything about Poplicola was thin: his frame, his hair, his eyes, his smile. He turned towards the podium.

'My lord Chairman,' he began in a nasal whine, 'esteemed Judges, men of Ostia, oh, and *women*, too.' Here he glanced at the defenders' bench and curled his lip very slightly. 'It is an unpleasant tale I must set before you today. A tale of greed and corruption. A tale of the foreign parasite that has wormed its way into our society and threatens to gnaw at the core of Roman virtue.'

He turned to look at Hephzibah. 'This woman, this slave, this atheist, this *Jewess* has committed the most terrible crime possible. She committed homicide. And it was not just any murder, but the murder of a Roman citizen. And she did not commit murder just once, nor even twice, but thrice! Yes, distinguished gentlemen. On three separate occasions she killed Roman citizens. Citizens just like yourselves.'

'Why, you ask, is one of the humiliores on trial? Should we not just crucify her and have done with it? Distinguished gentlemen, we can not. For she claims that her patron freed her before his death.'

Poplicola turned to face the dais. 'Yes. She claims that she is free. She aspires to be one of the honestiores. But really, gentlemen, can you see her as a respectable citizen? Look for example at the motley crew sitting beside her on the defenders' bench. They will give us a good indication of her moral values, for a person's character is often defined by the company they keep. I do not know them, but my friend and colleague does

I humbly give the floor to the esteemed magistrate, Marcus Artorius Bato.'

Marcus Artorius Bato was a short man with thin hair and pale brown eyes. Flavia knew he was intelligent, brave and honourable. On more than one occasion he had helped them solve a mystery.

As Bato rose from his bench, Flavia smiled at him and gave him a little wave. But Bato did not acknowledge her greeting. Instead, he turned to address the chairman and judges.

'Gentlemen,' he began, 'I do not know the defendant, Hephzibah of Jerusalem, but I know her friends and supporters. I have been invited to tell you something about them. As my esteemed colleague has just said, a person's character is often defined by the company they keep.

'Let us first consider the young advocate,' said Bato, gesturing towards Flaccus. 'At the age of twenty-five, the great Cicero considered himself barely ready to plead his first case. But I happen to know that this young man is not yet twenty. Still in his teens, esteemed gentlemen! And yet this "pretty boy Jason" plumes himself and dares to stand in this courtroom as an advocate.'

Flavia gasped and turned to Aristo. 'How can Bato say such things? Flaccus helped him rescue the kidnapped children in Rhodes! I thought they were friends.'

Beside her, Aristo gave a little shrug. 'It's the way things are done. Defamation of character is one of the lawyer's basic weapons. Think about it. If you can prove your opponent's friends and supporters are of bad character, then you've gone a long way to showing that your opponent is bad, too. And that gives you a much better chance of winning your case.'

'For example,' continued Bato, 'I happen to know that our handsome young orator enslaved a beautiful boy who was of *free birth.*'

'But Flaccus didn't know Zetes was freeborn!' protested Flavia over the scandalised buzz of the delighted crowd. 'And he set him free the moment he found out.'

'They always twist the truth,' whispered Aristo. 'It's part of their *modus operandi.*'

'I wonder,' said Bato, 'if the distinguished-looking old man sitting beside Valerius Flaccus is not perhaps our Emperor's long-lost elder brother, stolen by pirates in infancy.'

Lynceus looked startled, then pleased. The crowd laughed and applauded this witticism.

'That was not only amusing, but clever,' grinned Aristo. 'He's getting the crowd on his side, serving a tasty appetiser of gossip and humour.'

But Aristo's smile froze as Bato turned to him.

'Aristo son of Diogenes,' said Bato, 'is the curly-haired youth in the red cloak and ahem . . . rather short tunic.' He glanced at the judges: 'I won't even mention the fact that Hephzibah the Jewess seems to count some very good-looking young men among her friends.' Bato gestured towards Aristo. 'This handsome youth is a Greek, judges and gentlemen, a *Corinthian*. And we all know what is said about men from Corinth. I'm sure that young man has been up the Acrocorinth once or twice.' Bato raised his eyebrows knowingly at the judges, and smiled as he got another laugh from the crowd.

Flavia glanced at Aristo.

'All part of the procedure,' said Aristo. He still wore his stiff smile. 'I'm not taking it personally.'

Bato adopted a serious expression. 'But visits to the girls of Venus are trivial in comparison with what happened in May, only six months ago. I understand from my informants that young Aristo there was implicated in a brutal stabbing!'

Flavia gasped and looked at Aristo. He was no longer smiling and she saw a muscle in his jaw clench and unclench.

'Is *this* the kind of person the defendant counts among her friends?' said Bato, shaking his head sadly. 'And what of the woman sitting next to our defendant? Susannah bat Jonah. *Bat* Jonah? Not a very Roman-sounding name, is it? Although recently reunited with her husband, Susannah *bat* Jonah does not behave like a proper Roman matron. And yet this should not surprise us, for like the defendant herself, this woman is a Jewess, and until recently a slave. You may well recognise her, esteemed gentlemen of the jury, for she is often to be seen about town, barely veiled, without even a shopping basket or bath-set to give her wanderings some pretence. Where does Susannah *bat* Jonah go, and with whom? Perhaps it is best that we do not delve into such things.'

Flavia glanced at Jonathan. His face was very pale, and grew paler when Bato continued: 'Her son is the boy sitting on the bench behind her. Rumour has it that he started last winter's fire in Rome – a fire which killed twenty thousand people.' Here an audible gasp ran round the basilica, and then an angry rumble. The crowd was no longer cheerful.

Bato gestured towards Lupus. 'The boy sitting next to him might also appear familiar to some of you. Until recently, he was Ostia's resident beggar-boy and thief. He is mute, judges and gentlemen. Not because of any defect in nature, but because his tongue was cut out. I do not have to remind you that blasphemy is usually the cause of such an injury.'

'But not in Lupus's case,' muttered Flavia angrily. 'I can't believe he's saying such things. It's not fair!'

'I also know for a fact,' said Bato, 'that the boy who calls himself *Lupus* tried to hire an assassin last year. That little wolf was willing to pay to have a man killed.'

'Shame! Shame!' cried the crowd.

'As for the dark-skinned girl in yellow, she was a slave until the night before last, when she was hastily manumitted so that she would not have to give evidence in this trial.'

'Great Juno's peacock!' gasped Flavia. '*He* must be the one who told them about Nubia! How *could* he?'

'And last but not least,' said Marcus Artorius Bato, 'what about the young woman in the grey tunic and blue palla? What shall I say of Flavia Gemina?'

SCROLL XIV

Flavia felt her cheeks grow hot and her hands grow cold as Bato pronounced her name. 'Flavia Gemina,' said Bato, 'is the daughter of Marcus Flavius Geminus. A girl of equestrian class and marriageable age, she runs around Ostia unsupervised and unchaperoned, claiming to solve mysteries!'

'I am not of marriageable age!' protested Flavia, and would have stood and cried, 'You traitor!' at the top of her lungs, if not for Aristo's restraining hand on her arm.

'She pushes her rather large nose into places it really should not be,' continued Bato, 'and I would hate to say how much of your taxes she wastes when she calls upon magistrates like myself for assistance.'

Flavia felt her face grow hot with humiliation and rage, so she covered it with her cold fingers.

'There you have it,' she heard Bato say to the judges. 'If the moral character of a person can be defined by their friends, then Hephzibah the Jewess is a murderer, a woman of loose morals, an arsonist, a blasphemer, a slave and a meddlesome busybody. Do I need to say any more, judges and gentlemen? I think not!'

★

Bato resumed his seat, looking pleased with himself as he graciously accepted the compliments of those on the benches behind him.

Once again Lucius Cartilius Poplicola took the floor.

'Esteemed Chairman and Judges,' he said, 'my learned colleague has told you about the friends and associates of Hephzibah bat David. Now let me tell you about the defendant herself. First her pedigree, such as it is. She is a slave, to be sure, but not just any slave. No. As I said before, she is a Jew. A race of atheists, for they believe in none of our gods. Rebellious, too. Some would say the most rebellious race we Romans have ever conquered. Those of you who lost brothers, fathers and uncles in the rebellion not so many years ago will know the truth of this.'

A wave of applause rippled over the basilica and men cried out: 'Hear, hear!'

'One of the worst of those rebels was a Jew called Eleazar. A Zealot. An assassin. A sicarius. A man who vowed to stop at nothing to destroy the "Roman oppressor".' Poplicola turned and pointed at Hephzibah. 'It may interest you to know that this woman is his granddaughter!'

The crowd gasped and there were angry shouts from both men and women.

Aristo glanced around. 'I doubt,' he said drily, 'whether any of these people have heard of Eleazar before this morning.'

'Eleazar,' continued Poplicola in his ringing nasal voice, 'swore to stop at nothing until he had killed every Roman he could. And he made his relatives swear this, too! Rebellion is in this girl's blood, gentlemen. I will say it again: rebellion. And a murderous hatred of

Romans. And yet we bring such enemies into our midst. We let them prepare our food, dress us, bathe us, look after our sons and daughters!' Here he brought his hands up to his chest. 'We gather them like vipers to our very bosoms!'

An angry rumble rose up from among the spectators like thunder, then died away.

'Hephzibah the Jewess, granddaughter of Eleazar the Zealot and native of that rebellious city Jerusalem, sits before you today, accused of triple homicide. Do you know what all three of her victims had in common? One a rich recluse, one an honoured magistrate, one a hard-working merchant? Can you guess?' Poplicola paused for a moment, his left hand holding his toga, his right slightly upraised with palm open to the sky in the gesture of query. 'All three of her victims took part in the siege of Jerusalem. Each had a part in destroying her city and now *they are all dead*!'

As the crowd roared, Flavia gasped. She felt a strange sinking in her stomach, and for the first time she wondered if they had all made a terrible mistake: could Poplicola be right? Was Hephzibah a murderess?

Now Poplicola began to call witnesses. He called freedmen and tradesmen and even a decurion. All swore that they had heard Hephzibah vowing revenge against the men who had destroyed her city.

On the bench before them Hephzibah kept shaking her covered head, and once she turned her grave profile to Flaccus and Flavia heard her say, 'I have never seen any of these people before in my life.'

'What's happening, Aristo?' asked Flavia.

'I suspect those people have been bribed to testify against her,' he said grimly.

'Even the decurion?'

Aristo nodded. 'They must have paid an enormous bribe for his testimony.'

'But that's not fair!'

'They've probably paid people in the crowd, too,' he said.

'To do what?'

'To applaud and protest at the appropriate moments.'

'Can they do that?'

'They can.'

'Finally, gentlemen,' said Poplicola, as the decurion resumed his place on the prosecutors' bench, 'I would like to conclude my argument with a tale of bravery and cowardice. Even rebellious vipers can sometimes see the error of their ways. Let me tell you what happened at a place called Masada, a stronghold in the Judaean desert. Many of you will remember the terrible incident, for it happened only seven years ago. After the destruction of Jerusalem a thousand Jewish rebels fled to that desert fortress. For three years they hid, defiant and rebellious. But the power of Rome is invincible.' Here he struck his thigh with his right fist.

'After much hardship and great loss of men, our forces constructed a ramp and breached the walls. At this point the Jews did something which our great philosopher Seneca would have commended. They chose their own method of dying. They committed suicide. Yes, they decided to suffer death rather than face captivity and slavery. Even little children bravely exposed their throats to the knife, as a lamb to the priest. Nearly one thousand brave Jews, gentlemen. All died at Masada. All except seven. Seven cowards who hid like animals, afraid to meet death bravely.' Poplicola turned to look at Hephzibah.

'And that creature, that Jewess, was one of them!'

An angry rumble washed over the basilica.

But another sound cut through it, a cry like that from a wounded animal. It rose in volume, echoing in the vast space of the basilica and causing pigeons in the gallery to take flight.

The sound made all the little hairs on Flavia's arms rise up and at first she did not know where it was coming from.

Then as Hephzibah rose from her bench and tore off her palla, Flavia realised its source.

Hephzibah had fallen to her knees on the cold marble floor. As Flavia watched in horror, she ripped the neck of her dark stola and tore off her hairnet. Then she began tugging at her hair and scratching her cheeks. Hephzibah lifted her tearstreaked face and howled again. The crowds were utterly silent now, amazed and moved by the girl's expression of pure grief and pain. Many recognised the sound of a child who has lost a parent or a mother whose only baby has died.

Flavia felt tears sting her eyes and her throat was suddenly tight.

Presently Hephzibah's unearthly keening became a harsh guttural language. She was repeating a phrase. It sounded like 'Eye-kach yash-va-badad ha-eer, raba-tee am high-ta.' She was crying it over and over, and sobbing as if her heart would break.

Flavia saw Poplicola's startled face and realised he had not been expecting this. Abruptly, he came to his senses and angrily shook the folds of his toga. Perhaps this gesture was a secret prompt, for now hecklers were shouting again and crying out against the atheist Jewess.

Susannah was kneeling on the floor beside Hephzibah, trying to comfort her, but the girl would not be consoled.

Flaccus hurried to the podium and said something to the chairman. Flavia could not hear what he said, but she saw Gratus nod and turn to Praeco, who banged his staff.

'ORDER,' cried the herald, 'ORDER! THIS COURT IS ADJOURNED UNTIL TOMORROW MORNING AT THE FOURTH HOUR, ORDER!'

Hephzibah was so distressed that they had to hire a litter to take her back to Green Fountain Street.

Susannah walked on one side, Flaccus and his slave Lynceus on the other, Flavia and her friends took up the rear.

Flavia tugged the sleeve of Jonathan's tunic. 'What was she saying in the basilica? Was it Hebrew?'

'Yes. It was a verse from our ancient scriptures: *How deserted lies the city, once so full of people.*'

'Jonathan,' whispered Flavia after a short pause, 'do you think Hephzibah might have killed those three men? As revenge for them destroying her city?'

Jonathan shrugged, his head down. She guessed he had been deeply shaken by Hephzibah's grief, as well as the public reminder of his own guilt.

'I'd hate it if anyone destroyed Ostia,' said Flavia, and

looked around. The sky above was a pure exultant blue, a beautiful contrast to the orange-red roof tiles and the dark green tops of her beloved umbrella pines rising up from inner gardens and beyond the city walls. Even the rude graffiti on the walls was colourful and comforting. Up ahead, Ostian women stood at the green fountain, gossiping and laughing as they washed their clothes and filled their jugs.

'That's strange,' said Jonathan, suddenly lifting his head. 'How could a freeman like Mercator have fought in the Jewish Wars? Slaves can't fight in the army.'

'He could have fought as an auxiliary,' said Aristo. 'An archer or slinger, perhaps.'

'Unless Poplicola was lying about that, too,' said Flavia.

'Poor Flaccus,' murmured Nubia. 'He is very un-happy.'

'Did you see his face when she was crying?' said Jonathan.

Lupus nodded.

'Praise Apollo he had the presence of mind to get the case adjourned until tomorrow,' said Aristo. 'That was the right thing for him to do.'

Flavia looked at Flaccus's dejected back as he walked beside the litter up ahead.

'Poor Floppy,' she whispered to herself. 'Poor dear Floppy.'

They arrived home to their ecstatic dogs and to the sight of Flavia's father removing his toga in the atrium.

'Is the trial over?' asked Marcus, handing his toga to Caudex.

'Adjourned until tomorrow,' said Aristo, 'but it doesn't look good.'

'Oh, pater,' cried Flavia, 'it was awful! Bato the magistrate said all sorts of horrible things about us. And a nasty lawyer from the Poplicola clan almost drove Hephzibah mad with his accusations. You should have heard her wail.'

'That's what lawyers do,' said Marcus. 'It's why I never wanted any part of it.' He put his arm around her shoulder. 'Cheer up, my little owl! I've had some good news. You know I've just been to Cordius's will-signing ceremony?'

Still hugging him, Flavia nodded.

'Well, Cordius has bequeathed me and the other six a generous legacy.'

'What other six?' asked Nubia.

'Why, the six other witnesses, of course.' Marcus smiled at Nubia. 'Every time a will is drafted or redrafted it needs to be witnessed by seven Roman citizens. This isn't the first will I've witnessed, but it's the first one I'll benefit from.'

Flavia pulled away from her father's arm and looked up at him with concern. 'I hope you're not becoming a captator, pater.'

'What?'

'A legacy-hunter.'

'Oh course not,' he laughed. 'Cordius is my patron. I benefit from him alive, not dead.'

Nubia was touching Flavia's arm. 'Dead butterfly man said find other six.'

Flavia frowned at Nubia. 'What?'

'Your father is saying six witnesses plus him.'

Flavia looked at Nubia for another moment. Then understanding dawned in her eyes. 'Great Juno's peacock!' she cried. 'You're right! Papillio's last words were: *Find the other six*! Nubia, you're brilliant!'

'What?' said Marcus. 'What are you talking about?'

'Papillio – the man Nubia found dying on the stairs – said to find the other six. He must have been one of the seven witnesses of a new will.'

'What new will?' said Jonathan.

'Whose new will?' asked Aristo.

'Dives's! It has to be a later will of Dives!'

'But there *was* no later will,' said Aristo. 'If there had been, it would have come to light. One of the witnesses would have mentioned it.'

'Oh!' cried Flavia, clapping her hand over her mouth. 'Oh!'

'What?' cried Jonathan, Marcus and Aristo together.

'That's why he was killed!'

'What?'

'Papillio wasn't murdered because he witnessed Hephzibah's manumission. He was killed because he witnessed a new will. And the murderer didn't want anyone to know about it!'

They all stared at her for a long moment. Then her father shook his head. 'That's highly unlikely,' he said. 'If you wanted to hide the existence of a new will, you'd have to kill all seven witnesses. Plus the testator.'

'What is testator?' asked Nubia.

'The man who writes the will,' said Aristo.

'But the testator did die!' said Flavia. 'Dives died. And then Papillio and – oh!'

'What?' they all cried.

'The other man who was killed. Mercator. He was

143

one of Dives's freedmen. Pater, do testators often ask their freedmen to witness their wills?'

'All the time,' said Marcus. 'As long as they're Roman citizens they qualify. Three of the witnesses at the ceremony this morning were freedmen of Cordius.'

'Then that's it!' breathed Flavia. 'We've found the motive. Someone is murdering the witnesses of a new will.' She looked at them with wide grey eyes. 'If my theory is right, then five Roman citizens are in mortal danger!'

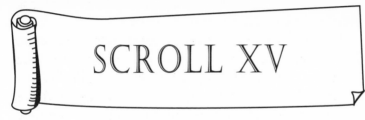

SCROLL XV

'If your theory is correct,' said Jonathan to Flavia, 'then where are the five remaining witnesses? Why haven't any of them come forward?'

Lupus drew his thumb across his throat and crossed his eyes.

They all stared at him.

'You think the murderer has already killed them?' breathed Flavia.

Lupus nodded.

'All five of them?'

Lupus grunted yes.

'Where are the bodies?' said Aristo. 'Apart from the two murders yesterday there haven't been any other deaths in Ostia. We would have heard . . . wouldn't we?'

'Shall I run to the forum,' said Jonathan, 'and ask the town crier if he's heard anything?'

'I have a better idea,' Flavia turned towards the kitchen: 'ALMA!'

'Flavia, don't bellow,' said her father. 'Go to the person you want to speak to.' He led the way out of the atrium into the inner garden.

'Yes, dear?' Alma was standing in the kitchen doorway, a half-plucked chicken in her hand.

'Have there been any other murders recently in Ostia?'

'Just the two,' said Alma, 'according to the women at the fountain.'

'Alma's fountain-friends always know the latest news,' said Flavia to the others. 'Even before Praeco.'

'Maybe they don't know about the murders yet,' said Jonathan, 'because the killer hid the bodies.'

'Or maybe witnesses are hiding alive,' said Nubia, 'being very afraid.'

'Why would they hide?' said Aristo. 'Do you think they know someone is trying to kill them?'

'Again, unlikely,' said Flavia's father. 'If five men knew their lives were in danger, chances are at least one of them would go to the authorities.'

'Maybe they don't know,' said Flavia. 'Maybe they don't live here in Ostia. Maybe Dives went down to the harbour and just chose strangers passing through. Or maybe,' she said, 'they were all travelling merchants, like Mercator!'

'The sailing season finished weeks ago,' said Marcus. 'Most merchants will be back in Italia by now. Unless they are based abroad.'

'Still,' said Aristo. 'It's worth investigating. Don't you think, Marcus?'

Flavia's father nodded. 'Yes. Yes, I do. I know the harbourmaster, and I know which baths he frequents. I'll ask him if he can get me a list of merchants who might have had dealings with Dives.'

'And I'll go to the basilica,' said Aristo, 'and see if there have been any deaths recorded recently.'

'If you see Bato,' said Jonathan, 'punch him in the nose.'

Lupus guffawed and Nubia giggled, but Flavia's mind was racing with the implications of her revelation.

'Flavia,' said her father, 'I know that look in your eye. I don't want you four charging around Ostia. Leave this to us men.'

'We don't have to charge around Ostia,' said Flavia. 'We only have to go next door. Hephzibah was Dives's slave for nearly a year; she might know the names of some of his freedmen and clients. Please, pater, may we go to Jonathan's?'

'Very well,' said her father, and kissed the top of her head.

'While you're next door you'd better tell Flaccus your theory,' added Aristo, 'before he falls on his sword.'

Flavia, Jonathan and Nubia found Flaccus in the dining room with his dark head in his hands. A plate of flat bread and white goats' cheese lay before him, untouched.

'Cheer up, Gaius,' said Flavia. 'We have some news. And here's Delilah with hot drinks for us all. Mint tea, by the smell of it.'

He did not lift his head from his hands. 'It doesn't matter,' he said. 'The case is lost. It's a total disaster. I've overturned my cart. What was I thinking, taking this on?'

'Don't say that!' Flavia took two beakers from Delilah's tray and set one on the table before him. 'We haven't lost yet.' She sat on a cushion beside him.

'Don't be a pessimist,' said Jonathan, sitting on Flaccus's other side.

'Gaius.' Flavia put her hand lightly on his muscular forearm. 'We know what Papillio's last words mean.'

Flaccus looked up at her.

'He said to find the other six,' offered Nubia.

Flavia nodded. 'We think he meant to find the other six witnesses to the signing of a will.'

'What will?'

'A more recent will of Dives,' said Flavia. 'We think Mercator was one of the other six witnesses Papillio told us to find, and that's why he was killed.'

'By Hercules,' said Flaccus, sitting up straight. 'You could be right. Only one witness is needed for a manumission, but seven are required to witness the signing of a will.'

'Pater and Aristo have gone into town to see if they can find any of the other witnesses, or a copy of a new will. And don't tell anyone, but Lupus is nosing around, too.'

'A new will,' repeated Flaccus, and stared at her. 'By Hercules! A new will!'

'Yes,' said Flavia. 'And if Dives left a new will, you know what that means, don't you?'

Flaccus nodded. 'It means we finally know who the murderer is.'

Lupus ran through the streets of Ostia.

The gongs had just clanged midday and the winter sun gently warmed the paving-stones of the town. As soon as it sank behind the town walls the air would grow cold, but for now it was perfect. Perfect hunting weather. A day so clear he could see every needle on the umbrella pines and every crack in every brick and every leaf on the pavement.

He had not eaten yet and his empty stomach sharpened his senses. Like a wolf hunting for its prey. Lupus felt the joy and excitement of the hunt fill his chest, and he grinned.

He reached the Decumanus Maximus, the main road of Ostia, and turned left, in the direction of the port. He dodged people on their way to the baths, heard the rattle of shutters being pulled across shop fronts, smelled the scent of roasting sausages and freshly baked break and spiced wine.

He passed the theatre on his right and the fountains and the square of the four small temples, and presently he came into the forum. There was the Basilica on his left, still with a crowd of men out front, though most were dispersing to make their way to the baths.

His sharp eyes caught sight of Poplicola at the centre of a crowd of men. Lupus ran to a portico and, keeping the columns between him and the men, he scurried from one to the next, approaching as close as he dared.

Presently he was near enough to hear Poplicola's nasal whine. 'I told you. Three sesterces. No more. Do the same tomorrow and you'll receive another three.' Lupus's eyes widened. Poplicola was handing out brass coins to the men standing around him. That man with the bald patch had been in the basilica. And that big African. And he also remembered seeing the man with the warts on his nose. Wart-nose had been yelling along with the best of them.

Poplicola was paying off the men he had hired to applaud.

'Who is the murderer?' cried Jonathan and Nubia.

Flavia opened her mouth but Flaccus cried, 'No!'

They all stared at him. 'I don't want to tempt the Fates by naming him,' he said. 'If we're right, we need more proof. Also, I want to talk to Hephzibah some more. I have a feeling there's still something she's not telling me.'

'Where is she, anyway?' asked Flavia, looking around.

'She's upstairs, distraught,' said Flaccus. He looked at Jonathan. 'Your father gave her a sedative. Then he went to try to find Miriam.'

'She's acting as midwife to that slave-girl at Nonius's estate.'

'Yes, we know,' he said. 'But poor Hephzibah was crying out for her.'

'If father gave Hephzibah a sedative, then we won't be able to speak to her for hours,' said Jonathan.

'Pollux!' cursed Flavia. 'We can't just sit here all afternoon! We've got to find out if there was a newer will.'

'Aristo told us not to leave the house,' said Nubia.

'I know,' said Flavia. 'Let's think it through.' She paced back and forth, then stopped and turned to Flaccus. 'Where do people keep their wills? Store them, I mean?'

'Many people keep their wills at home. But it's safest to keep them in a temple.'

Flavia nodded. 'If you were to make a will—'

'I *have* made a will,' said Flaccus softly.

'You have?' Flavia's stomach did a strange flip.

'I have made a will, also,' said Nubia.

'Me, too,' said Jonathan.

Lupus nodded and pointed at himself.

Flavia stared at then. 'You've all made wills?'

They all nodded.

Flavia sat heavily on the nearest bolster. Presently she turned back to Flaccus. 'But you're not ill, are you? Why did you make a will?'

'My father died last year. It's a Roman's munus – his duty – to make a will.'

'It's your duty to leave people money?'

'It's not about money or property, Flavia. It's about continuing the line. Maintaining the family genius. Honouring your ancestors.'

'So have you . . . Who have you . . . ?'

Flaccus smiled. 'I've made my cousin my heir. If I die, he will carry on the sacred duties to my ancestors. And inherit my Roman townhouse and my villa in Comum and most of my property and money.'

Flavia swallowed. 'And you keep it in a temple?' she asked.

'That's right.' Flaccus spread some goats' cheese on a piece of flatbread. 'At the Temple of Vesta.' He took a bite. 'In the care of the Vestal Virgins.'

'That round temple in the main forum in Rome?' said Jonathan.

'Yes. Many men of my class keep their wills there.'

'So Dives might have put his latest will in the Temple of Vesta in Rome?'

'It doesn't have to be the Temple of Vesta.' Flaccus reached to take a handful of dried mulberries from a glass bowl. 'It could be any temple.'

'That's no help. There must be a hundred temples in Rome. And that's not counting shrines or altars.'

'Shrines and altars are no good,' said Flaccus. 'You need a priest or priestess to look after your copy. So it would have to be one of the main temples, that is, one with priests or priestesses in attendance.'

Jonathan frowned. 'If someone dies, how do they know where the will is?'

'All seven men who witnessed the will should know,' said Flaccus.

'But in this case, two of them are dead and the other five are missing,' said Flavia. 'And we have no idea which temple it's in. Unless he stored it at his estate . . .'

'I could ride out to Nonius's estate and ask his bailiff,' said Flaccus, and then shook his head. 'But surely he would have told me when I saw him yesterday . . .' He took a thoughtful sip from his beaker. 'By Hercules!' he said. 'This mint tea is good.'

'Flaccus!' she cried. 'That's it! Papillio's last words. When he said *hercle!* he didn't mean the oath *"by Hercules"*, but rather *"in Hercules"*! He was telling us where to find the will. In the Temple of Hercules. Dives must have left his will in the Temple of Hercules! And we know exactly where it is, don't we?'

'In the Forum Boarium,' said Jonathan.

Nubia's golden eyes lit up. 'Pretty round temple by Circus Maximus?'

'Yes!' cried Flavia. 'One of us has to go to Rome now! We don't have a moment to lose.'

'But we promised your father we'd stay here,' said Jonathan.

Tigris barked and wagged his tail. A moment later Delilah appeared in the doorway.

'Your father and Miriam have just arrived,' she said to Jonathan. 'Miriam has gone up to be with Hephzibah and the doctor is in the latrine.'

Flavia turned to Jonathan. 'We need a copy of that will! You've got to convince your father to go to Rome, to the temple of Hercules. If he goes soon, he could be back by nightfall.'

Jonathan stood up and grinned. 'You mean if *we* go soon. I'm going with him.'

SCROLL XVI

Last will and testament of Flavia Gemina, daughter of Marcus Flavius Geminus, sea captain.

Flavia looked up from her wax tablet and scowled at Aristo, sitting across the table in her father's tablinum. It was late afternoon and he had returned from the forum with the disappointing news that the only death recorded in the past two days was that of a newborn baby.

'Do you have to sit right there?' said Flavia. 'This is private.'

'Yes, I have to sit right here,' he said mildly. 'If something were to happen to your father, then I would be responsible for you and your possessions until you marry. So I want to make sure you do it properly. Now remember: you have to name your heir in the very first line, or else the will is null and void. And with the other legacies, you have to use the formula "do, lego": I give and bequeath.'

Flavia sighed and took up her brass stylus again.

I, Flavia, make my dearest friend Nubia my heir. To her I give and bequeath my precious dog Scuto, all my clothing and jewellery, and any money I might have after payment of the legacies mentioned below.

To my dear friend Jonathan ben Mordecai, I give and bequeath all my scrolls and books, plus a gift of ten gold pieces.

To my dear friend Lupus I give and bequeath all my wax tablets and writing materials, plus a gift of ten gold pieces.

To my friend Polla Pulchra in Surrentum I give and bequeath my perfumes and make-up, plus a gift of ten gold pieces.

I would like to free my nursemaid Alma, so that she may become a freedwoman. To her I give and bequeath the amount of the slave-tax, plus a gift of ten gold pieces, if my father approves.

I would like to free our door-slave Caudex, who helped us in the arena in the first year of the Emperor Titus. To him I give and bequeath the amount of the slave-tax, plus a gift of ten gold pieces, if my father approves.

To the following people I give and bequeath a gift of ten gold pieces:

Gaius Valerius Flaccus, patrician and poet

Tascia Clio Pomponiana, daughter of Titus Tascius Pomponianus

Publius Tascius Pomponianus, also known as Vulcan, a blacksmith

Aulus Caecilius Sisyphus, freedman and scribe to Senator Aulus Caecilius Cornix

Scorpus, a charioteer for the faction of the Greens

Cartilia Poplicola, better known as Diana

Flavia looked at the ceiling and tapped her stylus thoughtfully against her bottom teeth. 'Who else,' she murmured. 'Who else deserves a nice legacy?' Then she gave Aristo an impish grin and wrote:

And last but not least, to Aristo son of Diogenes, faithful tutor and friend, I give and bequeath twenty gold pieces!

'There!' She looked at him.

'Very generous,' he said with a smile, 'but what about the cost of your funeral? And the upkeep of your family tomb?'

'Does that cost money?'

'Of course it costs money. Do you belong to a funeral club?'

'A what?'

'A funeral club. An organisation where you pay a few quadrans every month and when you die they give you a nice funeral.'

'Aristo. You know very well I don't belong to a funeral club.'

'Then you'd better add an amount to be devoted to that.'

'How much?'

'Do you want fragrant incense at your funeral, or just a few stale pine cones?'

'Fragrant incense, of course.'

'Garlands for the mourners and professional flute-players and a feast afterwards?'

Flavia nodded.

'A moving inscription on your family tomb?'

Flavia nodded vigorously.

'Then you'd better set aside ten gold pieces for your funeral and tomb.'

'Is that everything?'

'Yes. All you need to do now is put the date.'

Flavia nodded and wrote:

Written on this the seventh day before the Ides of December in the consulship of Titus Caesar Vespasianus Augustus and his brother Caesar Domitianus.

'I need to seal it,' said Flavia. 'I'll use the signet-ring I got for my birthday.' She twisted a signet-ring from her left forefinger. It was made of pale blue glass in a gold setting. 'See? It has a little Minerva on it.'

'Very appropriate,' he said with a smile.

'Don't I need to find seven Roman citizens to witness this?'

'No. Because you're still a child-in-power, this will isn't strictly legal. However, I would like you to seal it in front of me. That's it. Press it into the wax. Harder. Good. As your tutor I have the authority to confirm that it was done correctly and in my presence.' He wrote his name at the bottom of the wax tablet and pressed his own sardonyx signet-ring in the wax. Flavia knew it had the lyre of Apollo engraved upon it.

'There,' he said. 'If you should die before your father—' here they both made the sign against evil '— then at least he'll know your wishes. And if you outlive him you can make a new official will based on this one, with seven witnesses and the proper terminology. You might even ask a jurist to check it over. The tiniest lapse in legality can leave a will open to challenge.'

'Thank you, Aristo,' said Flavia. 'It was awful being the only one who hadn't made a will. Even though it's not strictly legal,' she added.

'Not quite finished,' he said with a smile. He reached into his belt pouch and brought out a tiny bronze box the size and shape of a fat myrtle leaf. 'This is a gift from me to you.'

'Oh, it's sweet! What is it?'

'It's a seal-box. Close the wax tablet. That's it. Now take a piece of string and tie it tightly around the tablet and the seal box – you have to open its lid – so that the box is on the outside of the wax tablet. Do you see the two tiny nicks in the seal-box, for the string to come out either side, like the nicks in the middle of the wax tablet?'

'Oh!' cried Flavia. 'I knew the little nicks were for binding the wax tablet with string, but I didn't know you could attach a little box, too! It's very clever.'

'You have to open the little lid before you tie it up and do the knot. See the tiny holes in the bottom of the seal box? When you drip in the hot wax, some of it leaks out through those holes and sticks it to the wooden outside of the wax tablet. But of course the string holds it in place, too . . .'

When Flavia had tied the string around the tablet and seal box, Aristo lit a taper of blue wax and dripped it in so that the liquid filled the box and covered the knot in the string. 'Now press your signet-ring into the wax. Quickly! Before it hardens. Good. Now close the lid of the seal-box to protect the seal inside!'

'Oh! I see!' cried Flavia. 'The only way to open the tablet now is either to break the seal or cut the string.'

'Precisely. Not even a hot needle will get us into this will.'

'A hot needle?'

'Some unscrupulous people have been known to open sealed documents with a red-hot needle, and then close them again. You can't do that with a seal box.'

There was a soft scratching and they both looked up

to see Nubia standing in the wide doorway of the tablinum. 'Hephzibah is awake at Jonathan's,' she said. 'Miriam says you may speak to her.'

Hephzibah was propped up on cushions with Miriam sitting beside her. It was dusk outside, and Delilah had just finished lighting the oil-lamp. Hephzibah's magnificent copper hair fanned out on the pillows behind her and seemed to glow in the light of a twelve-wicked candelabra.

Flavia and Nubia came shyly into her presence, while Flaccus waited outside with Lupus.

'Hello, Hephzibah,' said Flavia softly, 'I know it was horrible for you this morning. But we need you to answer a few more questions. Can you do that?'

Hephzibah nodded. There were dark circles under her eyes.

Flavia sat on the edge of the bed and took Hephzibah's hand. It was as cold as marble. 'Jonathan and Mordecai have gone to Rome,' she said gently, 'to try to find some evidence which will prove you are innocent. Flaccus is just outside in the corridor, with Lupus. He can hear everything, but he didn't want to intrude.'

'We've had a breakthrough,' came Flaccus's deep voice from beyond the curtain. 'But we need to know a few more things. You need to be honest with us.'

Hephzibah nodded, and then whispered, 'Yes.'

Flavia turned to Hephzibah. 'We need to know. Did you have an argument with Dives, your master, about a week ago?'

Hephzibah closed her eyes. 'Yes.'

'What was it about?'

'He asked me if I was from Jerusalem. I said yes.

159

Then he said he was sorry. I asked why. He told me . . . he told me he had been one of the soldiers who had besieged it.'

'Dives was at Jerusalem?' asked Miriam.

'Yes. Then he asked me if I had been at Masada.'

'What did you say?' asked Flavia.

'I said yes. Then he asked me if I had been there when I was a little girl. I just stared at him. He said he had been there, too. He was one of the two soldiers who had found us hiding in the cistern.' Hephzibah opened her eyes. 'He was the soldier who limped.'

'Great Juno's peacock!' whispered Flavia.

Hephzibah's brown eyes were filling with tears. 'Then he said that he and I were linked. That some god had brought us together and he wanted us to marry. I couldn't bear it any more. I screamed that I hated him and I ran out of the room.'

'And that's why you killed him?' said Flavia softly.

'I did not kill him.'

'But he was one of the soldiers who destroyed Jerusalem and Masada.'

'I know, but I did not kill him. The following day he summoned me again and said he understood how I might hate one of the oppressors of my people. He said he would not hurry my decision. He said he wanted to earn my love and prove he was sincere. Papillio was there – the man with the butterfly birthmark – and they set me free. The next day, my master was dead.'

'Why didn't you tell us he asked you to marry him?'

'Because it's too horrible to think about. He was so fat and old. And he was one of those who destroyed my city. Jerusalem the golden.'

'Do you realise that gives you a motive?' said Flavia. 'A motive for killing Dives?'

'But I didn't!' As the tears in Hephzibah's brown eyes overflowed. Miriam looked at Flavia reproachfully.

'I know Hephzibah would not harm the least creature,' she said.

'Hephzibah,' said Flaccus from beyond the curtain. 'Do you think anyone apart from the garden-slave could have overheard you when you had the argument about marrying him?'

'Perhaps. I was so upset. I ran out of his room, crying.'

'For example, was Nonius there?'

'I didn't see him.' Hephzibah blew her nose on a handkerchief.

'Tell us about Nonius,' said Flavia.

'I don't know much about him,' said Hephzibah. 'Just what the other slaves say.'

'What do they say?'

'That his father was a legionary in the Tenth, one of the legions that . . .' Here her eyes filled with fresh tears.

'We know,' said Flavia quickly. 'Go on.'

'They say his mother was from Syria. She and Nonius followed the father on campaign. I think Nonius's father was killed in the siege.'

'The siege of Jerusalem?'

'Yes. And his mother died of a fever a few years later.'

'I didn't think legionaries were allowed to get married until they retire,' said Flaccus from the corridor. 'I know they often have girlfriends and children, but they aren't legal.'

'I think,' said Hephzibah towards the curtained

doorway, 'that Vespasian honoured the children of the men who died in the siege by granting them citizenship, just as if their fathers had been married.'

'Did Nonius serve in Judaea, too?' asked Flavia. 'Like his father?'

'The army would never accept Nonius,' said Hephzibah.

'Why not?' asked Flavia.

'He is left-handed. Anyone who has lived in an occupied country knows there are no left-handed soldiers.'

'What is left-handed?' asked Nubia.

'It means someone who uses their left hand instead of their right,' said Flavia. 'We Romans believe that's bad luck.'

From the corridor Flaccus added, 'Even the word for left-handed – "sinister" – means unlucky and ominous.'

Miriam was amazed. 'Are you saying no left-handed men can join the Roman army because it's bad luck?'

'Actually,' came Flaccus's deep voice, 'the reason for not enlisting left-handed men is practical. In a Roman army, every soldier stands shoulder to shoulder with the man next to him. He holds the shield on his left arm, and half of it covers the man on his left, just as he himself is partly protected by the man on his right. A left-handed man would have to hold his shield on the right, and it would throw off the whole line.'

Flavia nodded at the curtained doorway then turned back to Hephzibah. 'So,' she said, 'as far as you know Nonius never served in the army. Never owned a gladius.'

'I don't think so,' replied Hephzibah. Outside it was quite dark and her face was pale in the flickering lamplight.

'And he was friends with Dives?'

'Yes. Because his father had been Dives's friend and tentmate.'

'That's right! Dives served with Nonius's father in Judaea! That's the link between Dives and Nonius.'

'Yes. Dives took Nonius in as a service to the dead father.'

'Is there anything else?' said Flaccus from beyond the curtain. 'Anything else you can tell us about Nonius? Anything at all, no matter how trivial?'

Hephzibah stared up at the flickering ceiling. 'He likes to count his money. He worships the god Mercury. He often loses his temper. And he refuses to eat brown bread, only white. That is all I know.'

'Does he have a wife?' asked Flavia. 'Or a girlfriend?'

'Or a boyfriend?' said Flaccus.

Hephzibah shook her head and closed her eyes. 'I don't think so. I think he only loves gold.'

SCROLL XVII

The funeral procession made its way slowly through the fog-shrouded streets of Ostia. Jonathan could hear the wailing before he saw it. Then the mourners emerged from the fog – like spectres – becoming more and more solid with each step. Presently he could make out Nubia leading the procession and playing her flute. Flavia and Lupus followed close behind her. On either side of the bier walked his father and mother. And behind them came the Geminus brothers, Marcus and Gaius, their heads covered by their togas.

Alma was there. And Caudex. But he could not see himself anywhere.

Was his the body on the bier?

The procession came closer and closer and just as he was about to see the face, he woke up.

But the bed was not his own. The room was too low and too wide. The sounds drifting in through the dark window were those of a city waking, not the usual dawn chorus of birds.

Then he remembered.

He and his father were in Rome. The previous afternoon they had visited the Temple of Hercules Victor in the Forum Boarium, but had found no will of Artorius Dives. They had also visited two temples of Hercules near the Circus Maximus. They had even visited the Vesta Virgins, but without success.

They would have to try other temples this morning, but they would not have much time. He knew if they could not produce the copy in Ostia in five hours time, the case would almost certainly be lost.

'Dear Lord,' he prayed. 'Please help us find Dives's will, if it exists.' But even as he prayed, he did not really believe his prayer would be heard.

Because of morning rites in honour of the god Tiberinus, Hephzibah's case had not been scheduled to resume until the fourth hour after dawn. Flavia and her friends duly arrived at the basilica two hours before noon, and found it almost too crowded to move. Aristo took a deep breath and began to shoulder his way through the excited crowd. Flavia, Nubia and Lupus followed in his wake.

When they finally emerged into the open space formed by the benches and podium, Flavia saw that Hephzibah and Flaccus were already sitting on the defendant's bench.

Flavia gasped.

The slave-girl's head was uncovered and her hair unpinned, as befitted a woman in mourning. It floated in a magnificent copper cloud about her shoulders. She was dressed in the same long black tunic she had worn the day before. The rip had not been repaired and it exposed her creamy neck and right shoulder. The stark black cloth emphasised her pale complexion and made her brown eyes seem huge. She had lined her eyes in dark kohl, which had streaked where she had been weeping.

Flavia thought she looked deeply tragic and utterly beautiful.

The judges filing to their seats obviously thought so, too. They were all staring at her open-mouthed, some bumping into those before them.

'Brilliant,' whispered Aristo. 'What a master-stroke. Play them at their own game. And to have Miriam sitting beside her. That should confound the prosecution.'

Flavia took a step forward and Miriam came into view, sitting beside Hephzibah. Her head was also uncovered, and her glossy black curls tumbled down out of a lavender scarf. She had also put on eye-liner and stained her lips light pink. Ripely pregnant and luminous in a grape-coloured silk stola, Flavia thought she had never looked more beautiful.

'What a pair of goddesses,' breathed Aristo. 'It's a shame I have to sit behind them.'

'At least you'll be able to concentrate,' said Flavia. 'Unlike the other side. Look at Bato and Poplicola.'

Lupus grunted and pointed at the lawyers on the bench for the prosecution, now also taking their seats. Nubia giggled behind her hand. 'They look like men having seen the head of Medusa.'

'But turned to stone by beauty rather than ugliness,' said Aristo with a chuckle. As they filed along the bench to take their seats, he bent forward and said in Flaccus's ear, 'Was this your idea?'

Flaccus nodded grimly.

'He's angry,' Flavia whispered.

'Yes,' agreed Aristo. 'And that's a good thing.'

Praeco the herald banged his staff for order and stepped forward:

'SECOND DAY OF THE TRIAL OF HEPHZIBAH BAT DAVID,' he blared. 'ORDER IN THE COURT-ROOM. ORDER PLEASE!'

Fat, bald Gratus rose from his bronze chair. The chairman did not waste time on preliminaries: 'The defendant has been accused of triple homicide,' he said. 'If this grave accusation can be proved – even in part – and if her status is confirmed as being that of a slave, it will be my duty to pass down a sentence of crucifixion.'

Flavia gasped and exchanged a horrified look with Nubia.

On the bench in front of them, Miriam took Hephzibah's hand and squeezed it. Hephzibah shuddered, but showed no other sign of emotion.

Praeco banged his bronze staff again. 'MARCUS FABIUS QUINTILIANUS TO SPEAK FOR THE PROSECUTION!'

From the bench opposite, Poplicola rose to his feet. 'Esteemed Chairman and Honoured Judges,' he smiled. 'I regret to say that my erudite and famous colleague Quintilian had to return to Rome. A family emergency. You will have to hear the proposition, proofs and peroration from me rather than him.'

The crowd groaned and Poplicola's smile froze on his face.

'That's good news for us,' whispered Flavia.

'And that looks like bad news,' said Aristo. He jerked his chin up towards the gallery.

Jonathan and his father stood looking down at them. One look at their faces and posture told Flavia what she needed to know. They had not found Dives's will in Rome.

★

Flavia looked up at Jonathan in the gallery above them. She gave him a consoling shrug and a smile, as if to say, *At least you tried.*

'Where is the Lupus?' asked Nubia.

Flavia looked around. 'I don't know. He was here a minute ago.'

'Oh,' said Nubia. 'There.' She pointed up. Lupus had just appeared in the upper gallery beside Jonathan.

'How did he get through this crowd so quickly?' said Flavia.

'Crawling through forest of legs?' suggested Nubia.

Up on the balcony, Mordecai was saying something to Lupus and shaking his head. Lupus looked dejected; he had obviously heard the news that the will was not in Rome.

Suddenly Lupus stood bolt upright and swung his right arm up from the elbow, his finger pointing to heaven, as if to say, *Wait a moment!*

Flavia and Nubia both watched with fascination as Lupus scribbled something on his wax tablet. Mordecai and Jonathan looked at what Lupus had written, then Jonathan nodded vigorously.

Lupus grinned and looked down at the girls.

He pointed at his head.

'He's had an idea,' said Flavia to Nubia. She nodded at Lupus and beckoned him on.

Lupus closed his wax tablet, held it up and made a circling motion, as if binding it with cord.

Flavia frowned, then her face lit up. 'The will?' she mouthed. She had shown them her bound and sealed will the night before.

Lupus nodded, then pointed towards the northwest.

Flavia and Nubia frowned at each other in puzzlement, then looked back up at Lupus.

The mute boy adopted the pose of a strong man in the palaestra, then pretended to wield a club.

Flavia was even more confused.

Now Jonathan entered in the mime. He gave a silent roar and made his hands look like claws. As Lupus pretended to strangle him, Jonathan obligingly sunk out of sight behind the parapet.

'Hercules!' mouthed Flavia. 'You're pretending to be Hercules!'

Lupus nodded and then, as a rather tousled Jonathan rose up from behind the balustrade, he pointed down, as if to say: *Here*.

'Oh!' cried Flavia. 'The Temple of Hercules here in Ostia!'

She placed the tip of her forefinger beside the edge of her thumbnail to make a circle, then held it up: the rhetor's symbol for 'Perfect!'

Lupus nodded happily, and disappeared into the crowd.

Flavia tapped Flaccus's muscular shoulder and he leaned back. 'Gaius,' she whispered in his ear, 'we've just realised something! The will doesn't have to be in Rome. It could be right here in Ostia. Lupus has gone to see.'

He nodded and sat forward again.

Flavia looked up at Jonathan, who shrugged his shoulders and lifted his palms skywards.

'What does he mean?' asked Nubia.

'I think he means we have nothing to lose by looking.'

Flavia brought her attention back to the floor just in time to hear Poplicola conclude his case against Hephzibah.

'Esteemed Chairman and Judges,' he was saying. 'I trust you will take into account the evidence we have presented and that you will condemn this girl.'

The crowd gasped as Poplicola pointed at Hephzibah not with his right hand, but with his insulting left.

'What is it?' asked Nubia, as Poplicola resumed his seat. 'Why do people gasp?'

'He used his entire left arm to point at her,' said Flavia. She had to speak into Nubia's ear because the hired applauders had begun to cheer loudly. 'It's a grave insult to point with your left hand.'

'I know,' said Nubia. 'In my country also, because the left hand is for wiping the bottom. But Hephzibah is not upset.'

'I know,' said Flavia. 'She seems very calm this morning.'

'I think what happens yesterday is good for her,' said Nubia quietly.

Flavia looked at Nubia. 'You mean when she broke down and wailed?'

Nubia nodded but did not turn her head. 'Sometimes,' she said, 'it is good to let go of pain inside.'

Flavia stared at Nubia's solemn profile, then gave her friend's shoulders a quick squeeze. 'You're so wise, Nubia,' she said. 'I always – Great Juno's peacock! That's it!'

Nubia turned her amber eyes on Flavia. 'What?'

'We don't need the will. I know how to prove who

killed those men! Gaius!' She reached forward and tugged his toga.

Flaccus leaned back again, one eyebrow raised.

'Gaius,' she said, her heart pounding hard. 'I think I've got the proof you need.'

From his vantage point in the upper gallery of Ostia's basilica Jonathan could see everything. He saw Hephzibah and Miriam sitting side by side. He saw the lawyers for the prosecution conferring and nodding. He even saw one of the judges picking his ear with the nail of his little finger.

Then he saw something he could hardly believe.

Gaius Valerius Flaccus, counsel for the defence, had stood up, turned around, taken Flavia by her shoulders and brought his mouth to her ear, as if to whisper something. But from his vantage point directly above them Jonathan could see he had not told her anything. Flaccus had kissed Flavia on the cheek.

SCROLL XVIII

Flavia's cheeks were hot and her heart pounding as Flaccus stood to address the Chairman and Judges.

'GAIUS VALERIUS FLACCUS TO SPEAK FOR THE DEFENCE,' announced Praeco, but he might as well have cried, 'GAIUS VALERIUS FLACCUS JUST KISSED FLAVIA GEMINA!'

She felt a wide grin spread across her face and tried to suppress it. She must appear suitably serious.

'Gentlemen,' began Flaccus his deep voice ringing with confidence, 'I know I have undertaken a burden in excess of my capacities, but I have done so trusting in your integrity, and in this woman's innocence.' He made a subtle gesture towards Hephzibah.

'The reason I accepted this case is as follows: I was approached by people whose friendship I value greatly.' He looked at Flavia, who was trying not to grin like an idiot. 'That young woman, Flavia Gemina, has been instrumental in restoring over a dozen kidnapped children to their parents here in Ostia. You yourself, Artorius Bato, can attest the truth of that.' Flaccus turned to Bato, who gave a half smile and inclined his head in assent.

'Flavia Gemina was helped in this good deed – and in many others – by most of those sitting on the bench behind me. My esteemed colleague has called them humiliores. Some of them may be humiliores in status, but in personal integrity, honour and bravery, they are all honestiores.'

This got a cheer from the upper gallery. Flavia looked up and saw Jonathan give her the rhetor's gesture for amazement. Then he wiggled his eyebrows and made a kissing shape with his mouth.

Flavia tried to scowl at him but her happiness would not allow it. He grinned back and jerked his head towards a hooded man standing on his left.

Flavia shook her head and frowned as if to say 'What?'

Jonathan hid his right hand with his left and pointed again at the hooded man.

Again, Flavia looked at the man. Then she gasped as she caught a glimpse of his eyes beneath the hood: they were as blue and sharp as icicles. The hooded man watching from the gallery was the great orator Quintilian.

'Nubia, look!' whispered Flavia. 'It's Quintilian, incognito!'

'In cog neat toe?'

'He doesn't want anyone to know it's him!'

'I believe,' continued Flaccus in his deep voice, 'that the opposition's case is a beggar's cloak of deceit, patched together with lies and scraps of innuendo, designed to hide the facts.'

'Nice metaphor,' murmured Aristo. 'And I believe it's original.'

On the bench in front of them, Lynceus turned his head and nodded. His eyes were twinkling. Flavia pointed up towards Quintilian. Lynceus nodded again, tapped the side of his nose, then put his forefinger to his lips, as if to say: Yes, I know; but don't say a word, understood?

Flavia nodded and turned back to watch.

'This morning,' Flaccus was saying, 'I intend to set the torch of truth to that cloak of lies, and burn the deceit away. All I ask of you, Esteemed Gentlemen, is that you resist the evil deeds of immoral men, and help me defend the innocent from distress.'

'What is he saying?' asked Nubia.

Flavia shrugged happily. 'I have no idea. But it sounds wonderful!'

Lupus reached the Temple of Hercules in no time. It was barely a stone's throw from the basilica. Could Dives have left his will here? Could it really be this easy?

At the bottom of the steps, Lupus closed his eyes and offered up a quick prayer.

Then he stared up the marble steps, making his way carefully between offerings of honeycakes, fruit and candles.

As he reached the top, he recoiled. A dead pigeon lay there.

Was it an offering to the god? Or just a dead pigeon?

He glanced round to make sure nobody was watching, then picked up the bird's light corpse and hid it in a fold of his toga.

You never knew when a dead pigeon might come in handy.

Flavia watched Flaccus with pounding heart and open mouth. He was magnificent. He had forgotten his Ciceronian quotes and his rhetorical flourishes. His gestures were almost as fluid and expressive as Quintilian's had been the day before. All eyes were on the handsome young orator as he launched a velvet-voiced attack.

'Someone wanted Dives dead, Esteemed Gentlemen. But it was not my client.' Here Flaccus indicated Hephzibah, who looked tragic and beautiful. 'Someone else stood to benefit not only from his death, but from hers as well. If we can find that person, Esteemed Colleagues, then we have found the culprit.'

Flaccus turned in a fluid motion and pointed dramatically at Nonius. 'You, Nonius, are that culprit, aren't you? You are the one who killed Dives, Papillio and Mercator!'

SCROLL XIX

Gaius Valerius Flaccus pointed an accusing finger at Nonius. 'You, Lucius Nonius Celer, called this girl to trial, but in fact you are the guilty one, aren't you? You suspected that Dives was going to marry Hephzibah. A wife does not automatically share in her husband's property, we all know that. But once married, the husband can name his wife as a beneficiary after his death. And of course there is also the question of children, that is, of proper heirs. When you discovered that your patron had secretly set Hephzibah free, you panicked. Why? Because you knew that a master often sets a slave-girl free before he marries her. And you suspected Dives was about to marry Hephzibah. The fact that he freed her secretly made you all the more sure of his intentions. The only point in his keeping her manumission a secret would be to keep the news from you and the other legacy-hunters.' Flaccus took a step closer to Nonius, who was glowering on his bench with his eyes averted.

'But you found out, didn't you? Perhaps you overheard it. Or perhaps one of the slaves told you, no doubt for a price. You knew you had to act fast. And so you killed Dives before any marriage could take place. Then, lest anyone suspect Dives's intentions and your motive, you claimed that Hephzibah was deluded and that she had never been freed. Perhaps you also wanted her under your control. And greed may also have been involved. Perhaps even lust. She is desirable, is she not?' Flaccus gestured towards Hephzibah and Flavia saw all the men in the basilica gaze at her open-mouthed. A slanting beam of late morning sunlight illuminated her cloud of copper-coloured hair and made it blaze like fire around her.

'You fool! If you had let the poor girl go free, you might have got away with your crime. But you reasoned that Hephzibah had not been at the estate long, and therefore had few friends or allies in Ostia. You assumed she would meekly accept your will. You didn't count on the determination of a young woman who has faced so many hardships in her life. You didn't count on Miriam bat Mordecai, a girlhood friend who decided to become her protector. You didn't count on four brave children and their tutor, all committed to solving the mystery.' Flaccus's dark hair fell over his eyes and he impatiently tossed it back with a flick of his head.

'But you did allow these four young truth-seekers to lead you to the witness, didn't you? Until that morning in the forum, you had no idea who Hephzibah's witness was. But then, when the town crier announced Papillio's name, you pretended to need the latrines.

'Instead you hurried to the Garden Apartments and there confronted Papillio. That was when you had your worst fears confirmed: Dives had not only freed this girl but he had secretly made a new will, which you feared would leave Hephzibah everything and you nothing. Papillio's dying words were: *I didn't tell. Quick. Find the other six. By Hercules.* What was it that Papillio didn't tell you? Who the other witnesses were? Where the will was kept? Whether he had left you anything at all?

'You didn't have time to beat the truth out of him because you had to be at the forum, to keep your appointment. But you had to get rid of him, first because he was the only person who could prove Hephzibah had been set free; second, because he knew *you* knew there was a new will. I imagine you used Papillio's own sword – he was an ex-soldier – then hurried back to the forum, leaving him to die a slow and agonising death.

'You wasted no time in trying to hunt down the other possible witnesses to the new will. An obvious candidate was Mercator, whom you knew to be a friend and freedman of Dives. You summoned him to your estate and took him to a secluded storeroom where you could speak uninterrupted. Did he tell you where the new will was? Or was he loyal to the memory of Dives? Perhaps we shall never know. What we do know is that you fought. I doubt a girl as frail and delicate as that one could have given you such a spectacular black eye. You and Mercator struggled, didn't you? And in the struggle he died. Did you intend to kill him, too?

'Whether you meant to or not, it was at this point that the solution came with terrible clarity. Kill Mercator and implicate Hephzibah in his murder. With her dead, even if the new will *did* come to light, the estate would revert to the heir of the previous will – you. You would then have nothing to fear from the other five witnesses. *If* you could just get rid of the girl.' Flaccus turned and gestured eloquently towards Hephzibah, whose flame-coloured hair was still dramatically illuminated by a beam of winter sunlight. She was visibly trembling and as she gazed at Nonius with huge brown eyes, she reminded Flavia of a beautiful doe facing the cruel hunter.

'You villain! You dragged the merchant's body to Hephzibah's cubicle, didn't you? Then you summoned her from the house of Gaius Caecilius Plinius Secundus, her protector. The innocent creature fell neatly into your trap.' Flaccus's toga slipped from his left shoulder and he impatiently pulled it up.

'It was a cold-blooded and brilliant plan. But you made one mistake. You underestimated the determination of this young woman and her friends.'

'There is no way you can prove any of that,' said Nonius. His good eye was blinking rapidly and his face seemed darker than usual.

A murmur ran through the basilica, now packed to overflowing.

'He's got it,' cried someone.

'It's the will!' cried a woman. 'He's found the will.'

'Ah,' said Lynceus, his eyes bright, *Lupus in fabula!* Speak of the wolf!'

The spectators grew quiet and in the hush, Flavia heard the slap of sandaled feet on marble. The crowd parted and her heart leapt as Lupus ran into the open space. His cheeks were pink and he was out of breath. But his eyes blazed with triumph. Behind him stalked a man in a long white robe and toga: a priest.

In his hand the priest held a wax tablet, bound with a scarlet cord and secured with a leaf-shaped brass seal-box.

'Please identify yourself,' said Flaccus to the priest.

'I am Gaius Fulvius Salvius, chief priest and haruspex at the Temple of Hercules Invictus, here in Ostia.'

'Do you store wills in your temple?'

'Yes. We do.'

'And is that the will of Gaius Artorius Dives?'

'It is. According to our records it was lodged with us last week.'

On his bench opposite, Nonius made a curious choking noise.

'Did you know that Gaius Artorius Dives died shortly after the will was deposited with you?'

The priest's jaw dropped. 'By Hercules!' he exclaimed. 'Did he? Is he . . . is Dives dead?' He licked his lips and looked around. 'I've been in the country celebrating the Faunalia and my wretched assistant . . .' He stopped then looked at the chairman and said in a clear voice, 'I'm sorry this happened, sir. Usually if one of our testators dies, a witness comes to collect the will and it is officially opened and read in the Forum.'

'May I?' Flaccus held out his hand.

The priest gave a little bow. 'Of course.'

Flaccus took the tablet and turned to the chairman. 'With your permission, sir, I will open the tablet.' He glanced down and added, 'I confirm that it bears the seal of Dives, which I have seen before: Hercules with his club.'

On his podium, Gratus nodded. 'I think we are all eager to hear the contents of his will.' The chairman turned to the priest. 'Thank you. You may sit.'

As the priest sat on the witness's bench, Lupus came to sit beside Flavia. Jonathan and his father arrived at the same time, having made their way down from the gallery.

The herald's bronze staff clanged, and Praeco's voice cracked with excitement as he announced: 'THE LAST WILL AND TESTAMENT OF GAIUS ARTORIUS DIVES!'

Flaccus broke the seal with a trembling hand. He handed the cord and seal box to a courtroom attendant and opened the wooden tablet. Flavia could see three separate leaves, each with black wax coating on both sides. A soft murmur of excitement spread through the crowd.

Flaccus quickly scanned the leaves and Flavia saw his eyebrows go up.

'This is indeed the will of Gaius Artorius Dives,' announced Flaccus in his deep voice. 'It is dated just over a week ago: the day before the Kalends of December, and it is signed and sealed by seven witnesses. He paused for a moment and Flavia saw that his hand was trembling.

'*I name as my sole heir,*' began Flaccus, '*Gaius Artorius Staphylus, my bailiff and freedman.*'

'What?' cried Aristo.

'Who?' said Flavia, and the basilica buzzed with excitement as others echoed their questions.

There was a hoarse cheer from the gallery and they all looked up to see a short bearded man in a white skullcap doing a little jig.

'Great Juno's peacock!' Jonathan had to shout to make himself heard above the crowd. 'It's Dives's Jewish bailiff. I met him at the funeral.'

Flavia gasped. 'That means Dives didn't make Hephzibah his heir after all!'

'ORDER!' bellowed Praeco. 'ORDER AND SILENCE!'

The basilica grew quiet and Flaccus's deep voice trembled as he read:

'*To Staphylus I give and bequeath my estate in its entirety. He will also receive the usufruct to the amount of one half.*'

'What is oozy fruit?' asked Nubia.

'He gets the proceeds from half the harvest every year,' said Aristo, and added. 'In this case, a great deal of money.'

'*One quarter of the usufruct,*' continued Flaccus, '*I give and bequeath to the synagogue of the Jews, for whatever purpose they see fit, for as long as that synagogue exists.*'

The crowd gasped and Mordecai exclaimed, 'Master of the Universe! Dives really was a righteous Gentile.'

'*The final quarter of the usufruct,*' read Flaccus, '*I give and bequeath to my freedwoman, Artoria Hephzibah.*'

An enthusiastic applause filled the basilica, Flavia saw Hephzibah and Miriam look at each other for a long moment. Then they hugged, and Miriam whispered something into her friend's ear. Flavia saw she was smiling but also weeping.

On the bench opposite, all the colour had drained from Nonius's face, making his swollen black eye look grotesque.

'Of course!' cried Aristo suddenly. '*That's* why Dives didn't name Hephzibah as his heir.'

They all looked at him and Aristo explained. 'If Dives had made Hephzibah his heir, the will might have been contested. She's a Junian Latin like you, Nubia, and her right to own property might have been challenged. But this way, she'll be rich for the rest of her life.'

'*Let all others for me be disinherited,*' read Flaccus and then looked up at the man leaning over the balustrade.

'*You, Gaius Artorius Staphylus, must accept this estate within the hundred days after my death.*'

'You can bet I will!' cried the man, and the crowd laughed.

Flaccus pressed on, '*But if you do not accept my estate, you will be disinherited, and my entire estate will be given as a legacy sub modo to the synagogue of the Jews.*'

'I still accept!' cried Staphylus, to an even bigger laugh. 'I accept it right now, in front of all these witnesses.'

Flaccus glanced up at him with a half-smile, then grew serious again. '*To each of the following citizens of Rome who witnessed this document, I give and bequeath a one-time legacy of 20,000 sesterces from my estate.*'

Flaccus glanced up at the chairman. 'Here follows the names of the seven witnesses, signed and duly sealed:

'*Cn. Helvius Papillio, a decurion of Ostia*
C. Julius Primus, centurion of the Legio X Fretensis
C. Messius Fabius, legionary of the Legio X Fretensis
M. Baebius Marcellus, legionary of the Legio X Fretensis
P. Valerius Annianus, legionary of the Legio X Fretensis
C. Artorius Mercator, cloth merchant of Ostia
C. Artorius Megabyzus, exotic animal importer of Rome.'

'That explains where the other witnesses are,' said Aristo. 'One of them is up in Rome and the other four are obviously friends of his from the army. They probably haven't yet heard of his death.'

'*Further legacies,*' announced Flaccus and the buzzing courtroom grew instantly silent. '*To those men and women who have so transparently sought my favour – my so-called captators – I leave five sesterces each.'*

'That part's the same as the earlier will,' said Aristo with a grin.

'Finally,' Flaccus had to raise his voice to be heard above the laughter and catcalls of the crowd, *'having discovered the true character and motives of my so-called friend Nonius Celer, I hereby leave him a piece of rope with which he may hang himself.'*

There was a moment of stunned silence. Then pandemonium broke out among the crowd: cries and curses interspersed with laughter and shouts of triumph.

'ORDER!' bellowed Praeco. 'THIS COURT WILL COME TO ORDER!'

'SILENCE!' cried Praeco the court herald, and his bronze staff rang out as he banged it sharply on the marble floor. 'SILENCE AND ORDER!'

The chairman Gratus added his voice, too: 'Order!'

When the courtroom was finally quiet again, Flaccus turned to Nonius, who had risen to his feet. The man's colour had returned, his face was livid with rage.

'It seems your patron passed judgement on you,' said Flaccus, 'as if from the grave.'

'There is no way you can prove I murdered Dives,' said Nonius, his good eye glaring. 'Or that I killed Papillio or Mercator.'

'I believe I can,' said Flaccus. 'Or rather, I believe this tablet can.' He tossed the will to Nonius, who caught it with his left hand and scowled down at it. 'How?' said Nonius, looking up. 'There's nothing on this tablet that proves I murdered anybody.'

'No, but the fact that you caught it with your left hand does,' said Flaccus. 'As my friend Flavia Gemina pointed out to me a moment ago, Mercator must have been killed by a blow from a left-handed man. Let me demonstrate.' He turned and gestured to Aristo.

Aristo stood hesitantly and as Flaccus beckoned again, he came forward into the open space, a faintly puzzled expression on his face.

'Mercator's skull was crushed by a single blow here,' said Flaccus, touching Aristo's head above the right eyebrow. 'Look how difficult it would be to do if you were right-handed, like most people.' He made a fist and swung his right arm across his body in a clumsy blow. 'Or even from behind. But our friend Nonius is not right-handed. He is left-handed. And look how easy it is if you are left-handed.' Flaccus made his left hand into a fist and swung it at Aristo, stopping just before it made contact.

In the basilica the crowd gasped with delight and broke into spontaneous applause.

Flaccus sent Aristo back to the bench with a manly pat on the back. 'Furthermore,' he continued, 'Papillio was stabbed by a gladius. But it was a clumsy wound. Why? Because the gladius is designed to be wielded by a right-handed soldier, not a left-handed man.' He turned to the chairman and judges. 'It appears,' he said, 'that Lucius Nonius Celer is a sinister man. In every sense of the word.'

The crowd roared enthusiastic approval of this witticism while the judges nodded and winked at each other.

But Flaccus was not smiling. 'Celer.' He looked around the crowd and waited for silence. Then he repeated the cognomen: '*Celer*. With his dying breath,

Papillio uttered the word Celer. He wasn't trying to say celeriter, "quickly"; rather, he was naming his murderer. That man!' Here Flaccus swivelled dramatically and pointed at Nonius Celer. 'That's why you fainted when you saw that Papillio was still alive and speaking to Nubia. That's why you tried to get her arrested and tortured, isn't it? Admit it.'

Nonius glowered at Flaccus for a long moment.

Suddenly something fluttered from the sky and thumped softly at Nonius's feet. He shrank back and a woman screamed. The lawyers on the prosecutors' bench shuffled to the ends of their seat.

'It's a dead pigeon!' cried someone.

Flavia looked up and saw Lupus gazing innocently heavenwards, as if to see from where a dead bird might have fallen.

'It's a bad omen,' shrieked a woman.

'The gods are angry with him!' shouted someone else.

Flaccus shook his head. 'How long, O Nonius, will you abuse our patience? How long? Come, sir. Admit your crime!'

Nonius looked down at the bird and then up at Flaccus. Finally he threw the tablet onto the marble floor.

'Yes!' cried Nonius. 'I killed them! I killed them all!'

SCROLL XX

'I killed Dives!' cried Nonius. 'I smothered that fat hypocrite with his own greasy pillow! He deserved to die!'

The court vigiles ran clanking towards Nonius, but Gratus waved them down with a command: 'Guard him,' he cried, 'but let him have his say. I want to hear this.'

The vigiles stood to attention either side of Nonius, but he seemed oblivious of them.

'That estate belongs to me!' he cried. 'My father died so that Dives could become rich.'

'Why don't you explain?' said Flaccus. His dark hair had flopped over his forehead and his eyes were bright.

Nonius turned towards the chairman on his dais. 'My father was the companion and tentmate of Gaius Artorius Dives. Brutus, as he was known in those days. Brutus the brute,' said Nonius with a sneer, 'not Dives the rich. They served together in the Tenth Legion, called Fretensis. They knew the temple in Jerusalem was filled with enough gold to pave the Via Ostiensis, and they were part of the very contingent sent to guard it. During their guard duty, the two of them hatched a plan. One of them would slip into the Temple and steal some small but valuable article. The other would keep watch. Artorius told me later that it was a bejewelled incense shovel he stole. It would never be missed. But it was solid gold and would make them both rich. Dives – or Brutus, I should say – quickly slipped this treasure into the neck of his tunic, then hurried outside again.

'Within an hour or two, some of the Jewish rebels set fire to one of the porticos. Meanwhile, my father had been ordered down to the lower level, but Artorius was trapped twenty feet high on the burning portico. He saw my father down below and he tapped his chest, so that it made a metallic sound. *"Lucius"* he cried out to my father, *"If you catch me, then I will make you my heir!"*

'As Artorius jumped, my father ran forward to receive him,' said Nonius, 'but the weight of Artorius's body crushed him.' He turned his tear-streaked face to the crowd and stretched out his hands. 'Dives lived, but my father was killed. I should inherit. It should be me! The riches are mine. It's not fair!'

Some of the spectators applauded but most were booing and a rotten lettuce narrowly missed Nonius and fell to the ground near the dead pigeon.

On his podium Gratus rose to his feet and gestured for silence.

'It is nearly noon,' he said, 'and time to adjourn this court. However, I believe we have heard enough. The judges will now vote on whether this woman is guilty or not.'

'How can he call for a vote?' whispered Flavia to Flaccus as he resumed his seat on the bench. 'Nonius just confessed to triple murder!'

Flaccus's jaw clenched. 'This hearing is not to pass judgement on Nonius, but on Hephzibah.'

'But they *must* vote not guilty!' cried Flavia.

'*Dum spiro, spero,*' quoted Lynceus. 'While I breathe, I hope.'

And Flaccus muttered. 'If they don't acquit her, I swear I will lose my faith in the Roman legal system.'

Flavia watched a court official pass out small tablets to the thirty judges sitting on their tiered marble benches.

'What are those?' Nubia asked Flavia.

'I'm not sure.' Flavia looked at Aristo.

'Those are voting tablets,' he said, and when Nubia frowned: 'Small wooden tablets with wax on each side. The letter A for *absolvo* – I set free – is inscribed on one side. On the other is a capital C for *condemno* – I find guilty. Each judge rubs out the letter he does not agree with, leaving the letter for the judgement he wants.'

Without conferring and in absolute silence, the thirty judges rubbed their tablets, then stood and filed past an urn. Each dropped his tablet into this urn. They all resumed their seats while a clerk tipped out the contents of the urn.

A deafening babble filled the basilica as two clerks checked and double-checked the vote. But an immediate hush fell as one clerk finally ran up to the podium and handed Gratus a scrap of papyrus.

The chairman stood and Praeco banged his staff. There was no need, for the basilica was now utterly silent.

'Stand to receive your sentence, Hephzibah bat David,' pronounced Gratus. Then he looked at her. 'You have been found not guilty by a unanimous vote. You are herby absolved of all charges. This court also recognises you as a Junian Latin, henceforth to be known as Artoria Hephzibah. Let no person say that

Roman justice is not blind to race or background: you may claim your legacy.'

'ARTORIA HEPHZIBAH IS ACQUITTED!' pronounced Praeco as the basilica erupted into cheers of joy.

'*Finis coronat opus!*' Lynceus clapped his hands gleefully. 'The ending crowns the work.'

'ORDER! ORDER!' cried the herald. 'THE CHAIRMAN HAS NOT FINISHED SPEAKING.'

The crowd grew quieter, though a low buzz continued.

'Lucius Nonius Celer,' said Gratus, 'you have confessed to premeditated murder in the presence of nearly a thousand witnesses. But unless a Roman citizen brings suit against you, I have no choice but to let you leave this basilica. Does any man here want to summon Celer to court? If so, the case must be heard in Rome.'

Several men ran to the base of the podium and waved wax tablets, with their formulas already sketched out.

'What have they got to gain by taking him to court?' Aristo asked Flaccus.

'Justice, of course,' said Flaccus, over his shoulder. 'It's not always about money.'

As the gongs began to clang noon, Aristo patted Flaccus on the back. 'Come on, friend,' he said. 'Let's get Hephzibah and Miriam back to Green Fountain Street. We all have some celebrating to do!'

Flaccus nodded and turned to Flavia, smiling. He was tousled and handsome and as he took a step towards her, she wondered if he was going to kiss her again.

But she never found out.

His smile had turned to surprise, for he was rising up into the air.

'Flaccus! Flaccus!' shouted the crowd.

Laughing, he twisted and tried to look back at them, but in a moment he was gone from sight, borne aloft on the shoulders of his adoring fans.

'The biggest mistake that Dives made,' said Flaccus later that afternoon, 'was trying to keep his latest change of will secret.'

They were all back at Flavia's house, drinking hot spiced wine in the triclinium. The children sat at the marble table with Hephzibah, while Mordecai, Aristo and Flaccus reclined on the dining couches. Lynceus stood discretely at the foot of his master's couch.

'And the biggest mistake Nonius made,' said Aristo, 'was assuming he knew what the new will said, and not bothering to find out.'

'I wish I'd been there this morning,' said a man's voice from the doorway.

'Pliny!' cried Flavia, and jumped up to greet him. Her father was still at his patron's house, so she was acting as hostess.

'I understand celebrations are in order,' said Pliny, and jerked his thumb over his shoulder. Flavia saw Caudex disappearing into the kitchen with a small barrel under one arm and an amphora under the other. 'I've brought chilled oysters and mulsum.'

Flavia clapped her hands. 'Alma!' she called towards the kitchen. 'Warm up Pliny's mulsum and serve it in our best silver goblets. Caudex, bring in the oysters as soon as you've opened them.' She turned to Pliny. 'Come in, Gaius Plinius Secundus,' she said, 'sit beside Flaccus in the place of honour.'

Pliny's dark eyes twinkled. 'I would be delighted to

recline beside the great orator Gaius Valerius Flaccus,' he said, 'but I would not claim one iota of his honour,' he said.

Flaccus laughed and grasped Pliny's outstretched hand.

'Do you know each other?' asked Flavia.

'Only by sight,' said Pliny.

'And reputation,' said Flaccus. 'I'm a year older than you, but I fear you're going to overtake me on the ladder of honours.'

'After today that won't be true,' said Pliny, stretching himself out on the couch. 'I hear you won a famous victory.'

Flaccus inclined his head modestly but Flavia noticed the tips of his ears were pink with pleasure.

'Tell me what happened,' said Pliny.

As Alma handed round silver goblets of steaming mulsum and Lynceus helped Caudex serve the oysters, they all took it in turns to recount the events of the morning.

'Fascinating,' said Pliny, at last. 'Fascinating.' He tossed an oyster shell onto the floor. Under the dining couches the dogs sighed deeply and stayed put; they knew oyster shells were not edible.

'What I still don't understand,' mused Aristo, 'is how Nonius knew that Nubia's manumission wasn't legal.'

'Bato must have told him,' said Flavia.

'But how did Nonius find out that Bato knew us?' said Jonathan. 'And so quickly?'

'Presumably he just asked clerks at the basilica if any of them knew who you were,' said Mordecai. 'Most of them know Bato sailed with you last spring.'

'Marcus Artorius Bato the lying weasel?' said Alma, as she topped up their goblets with mulsum.

'Yes!' said Flavia. 'Do your fountain-women have anything to say about him?'

'Indeed they do,' chuckled Alma. 'They say Nonius bribed Bato with the gift of a fine new townhouse on this very street. The lying weasel took possession of it yesterday afternoon.'

'That explains why he betrayed us,' said Jonathan.

'Traitor!' muttered Flavia.

Lupus nodded and angrily threw an empty oyster shell onto the floor.

Pliny sipped his mulsum thoughtfully, then looked up at Hephzibah, who sat at the table between Flavia and Nubia. 'If Dives had openly freed you,' he said, 'and let people know the contents of his new will, this never would have happened.'

Flaccus nodded. 'But Dives enjoyed the attention and gifts of legacy-hunters too much. He didn't want to discourage them.'

'That's right,' said Aristo. 'That was his fatal mistake.'

'But thanks to Flaccus,' said Flavia, 'Hephzibah will always be wealthy.'

Nubia gave Hephzibah a shy smile. 'I think Dives was loving you very much.'

'I believe it was guilt rather than love that motivated Dives,' said Mordecai. 'All his wealth came from an object stolen from the Temple of the Eternal One. By giving to you and the synagogue and his Jewish bailiff, he was returning what was rightfully ours. He was atoning for his sin.'

'I think it was a bit of both,' said Flavia, nodding wisely.

'We shall never know.' Flaccus cheerfully swallowed an oyster.

'Tell us, Pliny,' said Aristo. 'What brings you back from Rome? I thought you had urgent business there.'

Pliny looked round at them, then dropped his head. 'I was a coward,' he said. 'I heard that Quintilian was arguing for the prosecution, and I was afraid to go up against him. It is to my eternal shame.' He looked up at Flaccus. 'Do you know that he sought me out in Rome yesterday and said he had seen a promising young lawyer pleading a most fascinating case in Ostia's basilica.'

'Oh,' groaned Flaccus. 'I was terrible yesterday. I made all the mistakes of a tiro.'

'But you were brilliant today,' said Flavia. 'And guess what? Quintilian was there! He was up in the gallery watching you.'

'Was he?'

'It's true,' said Jonathan. 'I was standing right next to him. He kept saying things like *"well done"* and *"brilliant"*.'

'Did he really?' Flaccus's ears grew pink again.

'I wish I'd seen you in action,' said Pliny. 'I must confess, I'm sick with jealousy. But I shall do the noble thing. If you like, I will introduce you to him.'

'To Quintilian?' said Flaccus, choking on a sip of mulsum.

'To Marcus Fabius Quintilian himself. I'll even suggest he take you on as an assistant.'

'Would you really put in a word for me?' said Flaccus. 'To study with such a master . . .'

'Of course I will. And I insist that you come back with me this evening and spend the night at my Laurentine villa and tell me all about yourself. If your hosts don't mind,' he added.

'I mind,' said Flavia. Then she sighed and smiled at Flaccus, 'But I give you permission to depart.'

'Thank you, Flavia,' said Flaccus with a heart-stopping smile. He turned to Lynceus. 'Pack our things?'

Lynceus nodded and disappeared upstairs.

'Tell me, Artoria Hephzibah,' said Pliny, 'What will you do with your new-found wealth?'

'I hope to buy your Laurentum Lodge,' she said softly.

'What?' Pliny stared. 'My little lodge? Why, you could buy an estate twice as big as mine with your new-found riches.'

Hephzibah shook her head. 'If you sell me the Lodge, I will give it to Miriam and Gaius.' Hephzibah lowered her head. 'All I want is to live with Miriam and help her raise her children.' She began to weep softly.

'Don't cry,' said Pliny. 'I'll sell you the Lodge. I'll give you a good price, too.'

'She's just tired,' said Flavia, slipping an arm around Hephzibah's shoulder. 'She's been through so much.'

'Where is Miriam, anyway?' asked Pliny, looking around. 'I expected she'd be celebrating with you.'

'Miriam's resting at our house, in her old bedroom,' said Jonathan.

Mordecai smiled. 'I think, Hephzibah, that we should take you next door. You could probably use a nap, too. And then we will welcome in the Sabbath together.'

Lynceus appeared in the tablinum doorway; he was

holding Flaccus's satchel. As they all rose from couch and chair, there was a soft but urgent knock on the door. The dogs ran barking towards the atrium. A moment later Delilah appeared in the wide doorway of the dining room, with Caudex close behind her.

'Master,' she said to Mordecai. 'It is your daughter, Miriam. Her time has come!'

Pliny turned to the doctor. 'Do you want us to take her home, to the Laurentum Lodge?' he asked. 'I have a well-sprung carruca outside.'

'No,' said Mordecai. 'It's better if she has the baby here, under my supervision. But if you and Flaccus are going back now, will you stop by the Lodge and tell Gaius to come at once?'

SCROLL XXI

Flavia's uncle Gaius arrived at Jonathan's house within the hour. He joined Nubia and Flavia and the others in Mordecai's tablinum. Presently Marcus arrived, too, back from Cordius's house. The two brothers went next door to make an offering at the Geminus family lararium, then returned to join the vigil.

At around midnight, Nubia and Flavia went up to Miriam's room to see if they could help. Miriam sat on the birthing chair, with her mother and Hephzibah offering encouragement.

Not once did Miriam cry out but Nubia could see the pain on her lovely face. Her glossy curls were damp with sweat and she was trembling with exhaustion. Presently they had to help her from the birthing stool to the bed. Nubia and Flavia sponged Miriam's forehead. Susannah held her daughter's hand and whispered words of love and encouragement. Hephzibah rocked gently and prayed in her own language. Delilah came in and out, bringing spiced wine or posca or snacks. But nothing tempted Miriam.

Finally, at first cockcrow Susannah looked up at the girls. 'Bring my husband. There is something wrong.'

Mordecai came at once, and bent over his daughter.

'No, father, you should not see me like this,' whispered Miriam. Her hair was damp and her eyes were dark with pain.

'Shhh, my daughter. It does not displease the Lord. This is my calling from him, to heal and bring new life.'

But Nubia saw his face darken as he examined his daughter's distended belly. And she saw the anguished look he gave his wife.

'Twins,' he said. 'Why didn't you tell me?'

'What could you have done?' Susannah replied.

'Miriam,' said Mordecai. 'I may not be able to save them. If you are to live . . .'

'No, father,' whispered Miriam fiercely. 'My sons must live. The Lord told me. They must live!'

'My daughter, listen to me. Their position is wrong. You can have others. And how would these survive without a mother? Who will feed them?'

'No!' cried Miriam. She pushed herself up onto her elbows and Nubia saw the beads of sweat on her forehead and upper lip. 'My babies must live! Swear you will save them, at any cost.'

'Our Lord tells us not to make vows: "Let your yes be yes and your no"—'

'Swear it!' cried Miriam fiercely. 'Swear it!'

In a heartbeat of silence Nubia heard a cock crow in the night. Dawn was not far off.

'I swear it,' said Mordecai at last, and handed a cylindrical leather case to Nubia. 'Reach into my capsa,' he said, 'and find the poppy tears. I do not want her to suffer any more than she has to.'

*

Jonathan sat in the cinnamon-scented tablinum and stared at a flickering oil-lamp. Beside him Lupus was asleep. On the divan next to him Gaius and Marcus sat in silence, absorbed in their fears and memories. Jonathan remembered that Flavia's mother had died in childbirth and he closed his eyes.

'Dear Lord,' he prayed silently. 'Please let Miriam live. And her baby, too. Let them both live and I promise I will serve you and obey you and never abandon you again. Just let them live.'

The roosters began to crow again, this time with more conviction, for the square of sky above the garden was no longer black, but charcoal grey. Dawn was not far off.

Then he heard another sound. A sound that made him stifle a sob of joy. It was the stuttering cry of a newborn baby: indignant, demanding and full of strength.

Gaius and Marcus exchanged a look and for the first time that night Jonathan saw them smile.

But their smiles faded when the cry of a second newborn joined the cries of the first.

'Twins!' whispered Marcus, and he pronounced the words like a death-sentence. 'May the gods be merciful. It's twins.'

They were all three on their feet now, moving to the wide doorway of the tablinum, looking up towards Miriam's room.

It seemed like an aeon, but the sky was still grey, so it could only have been a few minutes when they heard the sound of brass curtain rings sliding along a wooden rod. A moment later, Flavia and Nubia appeared on the balcony. Each held a small, pale bundle: a twin wrapped in swaddling clothes. They came slowly down the polished wooden stairs, infinitely careful of their precious burdens. In the flickering torchlight, Jonathan saw that although their faces were pale with fatigue, their eyes were shining.

Flavia and Nubia shyly went into the tablinum and each put a baby carefully down on the floor at Gaius's feet. With a low cry, he bent and took both twins onto his knees.

A creak on the stairs made Jonathan turn. Hephzibah was coming furtively down, her face blank with grief.

Jonathan looked at Gaius, and at the girls cooing over the twins. They didn't know. But Hephzibah did.

'No!' cried a voice, and when they all looked at Jonathan he realised the voice had been his.

Hephzibah covered her head with her palla and ran weeping through the courtyard and into the atrium. A moment later Jonathan heard the front door open and then close behind her.

Then another dark figure appeared on the balcony above them. It was Mordecai. His face, lit from below by the torchlight, was full of anguish, too.

'She wants to see you, Gaius. Quickly. There isn't much time.'

At dawn on the second Sabbath of December the residents of Green Fountain Street heard the unmistakable sounds of mourning coming from the house where the Jewish family lived. Women going to the fountain, men eating a hasty chunk of bread, children packing their satchels for school all stopped as they heard the wails of grief mingled with the cries of hungry newborns. Women hugged their daughters, and mothers clutched their babies, and all made the sign against evil. For every one of them knew what the cries meant.

In the house of the Jews, a young woman had died in childbirth.

SCROLL XXII

*L*ast will and judgement of Miriam bat Mordecai.

Dearest Gaius, I make you the heir of all I have. I am so sorry that I have left you. And I am sorry that I have left my sons. How I wish I could see them grow up. But I am full of hope. For the Lord told me they would do great things. He sent his messenger to me: an angel, Gaius, an angel!

The messenger came to me last month. A giant with wings, in white garments so bright I could hardly gaze upon them. I was terrified. How I trembled. But he told me not to be afraid. And when he spoke, the babies stirred in my womb. 'Will you come?' said the angel, and his voice sounded like the rushing waters of a river when it floods in the winter. I tried to answer, but my tongue was too dry. 'Will you come?' he repeated. Again I tried to answer and again I could not. 'Will you come?' he said for a third time. This time I nodded. He smiled and held out his hand. I took it. Then – and I can hardly believe it myself – he lifted me up into the sky.

Gaius, dear Gaius, as he lifted me up I saw Ostia from above, the way a bird must see it. I saw the Tiber, winding like a silver ribbon to the sea as blue as sapphires. I saw my father's house with its tiny garden courtyard. I saw the theatre and the forum and the lighthouse with its plume of dark smoke. And people like ants, so colourful, so busy, so dear to their Creator. And then I was too high to see them anymore. For I was above the clouds and I thought I should faint but he spoke a word which strengthened me.

And then, Gaius, then the angel lifted me up to paradise. And oh, Gaius! If I could only tell you how wonderful it was! But even were it permitted, words cannot describe its beauty.

'Why are you showing me this?' I asked the angel.

'To help you,' he replied, 'when the time comes for the sacrifice.'

'We do not sacrifice any more,' I told him. 'Our Lord was the final sacrifice, once and for all people.'

The angel smiled. 'Yes,' he said, and then he added. 'Your sons will do great things. Trust in the Lord always.'

Gaius, if it is acceptable to you, will you give the twins the names 'Soter' and 'Philadelphus'? I believe they will save many. This is my last will and wish.

Dear Gaius, I have not regretted one moment of our time together. To you and to my family and to my friends and to my sons I give my love. It is all I have to give. My legacy is love.

Witnessed by Hephzibah bat David on this the Nones of November, in the second year of the Emperor Titus.

Gaius slammed the wax tablet onto the octagonal table. 'She wrote this over a month ago!' he said to Mordecai, his voice hoarse from crying out to the gods. 'She knew! And so did Hephzibah!'

'Where is Hephzibah?' whispered Flavia. She was holding a crying twin and trying to comfort him. 'Hephzibah said she would help with the children and now she's needed more than ever.'

'She ran away,' said Jonathan flatly. 'I don't think she could face it.'

Flavia saw that his eyes were red-rimmed with weeping. She was exhausted, too, with grief and fatigue. She rocked the wailing baby, and shushed him, but he was hungry and would not be comforted.

'Here, Nubia,' Flavia handed over the tiny squalling bundle. 'You try for a while.'

Nubia began singing to the baby in her own language, and his cries lessened a little so that Flavia was able to hear a knock at the front door. Tigris heard it, too. He silently rose to his feet and padded out of the room. Flavia followed him into the brightening atrium. When she reached the front door, she slid open the peephole.

It was Hephzibah, standing in the porch with two young women. All three were wrapped in their pallas and shivering in the cool of dawn. Flavia opened the door and stood back. Without a word, Hephzibah led the two women through the atrium and Flavia followed. They went straight to the tablinum, where Nubia and Susannah were still trying to calm the twins.

'I have brought Lydia and Priscilla,' said Hephzibah. 'Miriam made arrangements for them to be wet-nurses.'

'What?' said Gaius. 'She what?'

Everyone stared as the smaller, fair-haired girl snatched one of the crying twins from Susannah's startled arms. As they watched, the girl sat on the divan and urgently hid the crying baby behind her palla. A moment later the baby was silent and the girl closed her eyes in something like ecstasy.

The other girl, who was taller and darker, handed Flavia a bundle and took the other twin from Nubia's arms. She sat beside the first girl and opened her palla and presently the second twin was silent, too.

'Lydia and Priscilla will be wet-nurses for the twins,' explained Hephzibah. 'Lydia lost her own baby a few days ago and Priscilla has just had a little girl.'

Flavia looked down at the bundle in her arms. It was a tiny baby with crumpled face and a mop of dark hair, tightly swaddled.

'Praise the Lord!' whispered Susannah, and she began to weep.

'But how?' said Gaius. 'When?'

'Miriam bought Lydia last week,' said Hephzibah. 'She used some of her dowry money. And Priscilla's new owner Staphylus would not accept even one sestertius in payment. He says that without us he wouldn't be the owner of the richest estate in Laurentum. He says that Priscilla and her baby are his gift to us.' Hephzibah sat between the girls and put an arm around each.

The fair-haired girl – Lydia – looked at Hephzibah, her face was wet with tears but her eyes shone with joy. 'He's feeding,' said Lydia. 'He's feeding.'

'Yes,' said Hephzibah. 'These twins will live. They have a destiny.'

On the morning of the funeral, Jonathan watched them carry his sister's body on a bier through the streets of Ostia. He had been to the Jewish quarter to tell his father's relatives the news, and now he was about to rejoin the procession. It was a foggy day, and the red-brick walls of the town were damp and dripping.

It was not a long procession, for she had not been famous or rich. She was just another young mother claimed by childbirth, as so many were. But on the painted statues of the town, the moisture condensed and dripped so that the gods seemed to weep along with the mourners.

Jonathan watched the scene from his dream in anguish. She was dead. His lovely sister was dead.

'Why, Lord?' whispered Jonathan. 'Why did you show me this? What could I have done?'

He was just about to step forward to join the procession when he felt a man's presence behind him. He could sense the man's sorrow and compassion. He did not dare turn around.

'Why, Lord?' he repeated.

'So that you can encourage others,' said the man's voice.

'How?'

'When you stand before the tomb,' said the man, 'the words will be given to you.'

Jonathan could not help himself; he turned around.

But there was no one there.

Jonathan's father and Gaius were so crippled with grief that they could not carry the bier. Marcus and Caudex took the front, with Senex and Dromo carrying the back. Nubia led the procession – playing her flute – with Flavia on one side and Lupus on the other. Susannah, Delilah, Hephzibah and the two young wet-nurses followed behind, together with most of the relatives who had been at Miriam's betrothal supper. Jonathan moved forward and fell into step beside Lupus.

As the procession made its way through the streets towards the Laurentum Gate, some people emerged from their shops to see who had died. But most were busy with their preparations for the Saturnalia and remained indoors. They were unwilling to taint the promise of a joyful festival with the ill-omened sight of a young woman's funeral.

The procession turned right out of the Marina Gate, and trudged along the sand dunes towards the river, where a hooded ferryman waited to take them across to the tombs of the Isola Sacra. For a time they were floating in grey nothingness, with no sound apart from the plop of the oars, the sobs of mourners and Nubia's plaintive flute. Then they were across, and at last they placed her before the tomb. Her body had been anointed with myrrh and aloes, then wrapped in strips of linen. Her bandaged hands held her favourite doll.

Flavia and Nubia clung to each other and wept. Lupus stood apart, looking damp and miserable, for he had refused to wear a cloak. Gaius was crying out against the gods. His brother Marcus stood silently beside him, bleak with the memories of his own loss eight years earlier. Hephzibah stood quietly, carefully and methodically cutting her hair with shears, letting it fall to the ground. Nearby, Alma, Lydia and Priscilla each held a sleeping baby.

There were a few other Ostians already there. Staphylus and Restituta. Pistor the baker, and his family. Diana Poplicola and her mother Vibia. And between the fog-shrouded tombs to his left Jonathan thought he saw a flicker of red. Aristo?

He realised that Nubia had stopped playing her flute and was looking at him expectantly. The cries of the mourners had ceased, now, too.

Jonathan looked at his father, whom he had expected to give the eulogy. But Mordecai was half-crouched in a patch of damp grass, whimpering like an animal in pain. Susannah knelt beside him, murmuring words of comfort. Nearby, Gaius's eyes were closed and his face lifted and his mouth open in a silent howl.

Jonathan stepped forward. He knew it was up to him.

'We have come to bid Miriam farewell,' he began, but his voice was swallowed by the fog.

He began again, this time speaking from his diaphragm as he had seen Flaccus do.

'Miriam was a sister, wife, daughter, mother and friend,' he said. This time his voice carried and they all grew quiet and looked at him. Only Mordecai continued to whimper quietly.

'Miriam saw paradise,' said Jonathan. 'An angel showed her. She was ready to go, for although she loved this world, she also longed for the next one.' He looked around at them. 'Can you imagine that? She *longed* for the next. Already in her heart, she was there.'

Gaius cried out to the sky, but presently his howl subsided into a sob and after a moment he bowed his head and was quiet.

Jonathan looked at Flavia. Her eyes were filled with tears, but she nodded back at him and mouthed the words: 'Go on.'

He took a deep breath and resumed. 'Our Messiah once said this: *You have seen and so you believed*. Miriam saw paradise, and so she believed. But not many people are given a sight of the next world. How can you be assured? Or how can I? Only through faith. For the same Lord said, *Blessed are you who have not seen, and yet have believed*.

Jonathan gestured towards the slender body in its

myrrh-scented wrapping. 'In a moment we will lay her to rest in that tomb,' he said. 'But that is not the end. For Miriam believed in the resurrection of the dead. She died in the faith that one day she will come back out of that tomb and be taken to a wonderful place. She will meet her sons there. And us, too, if we can only grasp the crown as she did.'

He looked around at them. Mordecai and Gaius still had their heads bowed. But Flavia, Nubia and Lupus were watching him with shining eyes, and this gave him strength.

'Her death is a tragedy,' continued Jonathan, 'but also a triumph. A triumph of faith and love. For she made the ultimate sacrifice. She gave her life so that her babies would live. And just as the nine months they spent in her womb were their preparation for this life, so the fifteen years Miriam spent on earth were her preparation for the next. She has run her race and soon she will claim her reward.'

Jonathan looked around at the mourners. 'Some of you do not believe in our God,' he said, 'or in our faith, or in the resurrection of the dead. But many of you admire the great Roman philosopher Seneca. Perhaps his words will comfort you. He said, *Only after our death do we know if we've had a good life.*'

Jonathan paused, then took a deep breath. 'Miriam's life was not just a good life,' he said, and although tears were now running down his cheeks, he smiled, 'it was the best life.'

FINIS

ARISTO'S SCROLL

Acrocorinth (uh-*krok*-oh-rinth)
  dramatic mountain which rises above Corinth; it was the
  site of a sanctuary and the notorious temple of Aphrodite,
  with its beautiful priestesses
aedile (*eye*-deel)
  in Ostia two aediles were chosen each year to oversee
  upkeep of public buildings like temples and markets; they
  also supervised weights and measures
amphitheatre (*am*-fee-theatre)
  oval-shaped stadium for watching gladiator shows, beast
  fights and the execution of criminals
amphora (*am*-for-uh)
  large clay storage jar for holding wine, oil or grain
atrium (*eh*-tree-um)
  the reception room in larger Roman homes, often with
  skylight and pool
Augustus (awe-*guss*-tuss)
  Julius Caesar's adopted nephew and first emperor of
  Rome, died in AD 14
basilica (ba-*sill*-ik-uh)
  large public building in the forum of most Roman
  towns, it served as a court of law and meeting place for
  businessmen; you can still see remains of Ostia's basilica

Brundisium (brun-*dee*-zee-um)
(modern Brindisi) a port on the heel of Italy

capsa (*kap*-sa)
cylindrical leather case, usually for holding scrolls or
medical implements

captator (kap-*tat*-or)
word coined by the poet Horace to mean a legacy-
hunter; literally means a fisher or hunter

carruca (ka-*roo*-kuh)
four-wheeled travelling carriage, usually mule-drawn and
often covered

Cassandra (kass-*and*-rah)
mythological princess and prophetess of Troy; she was
cursed by Apollo so that she could always forsee the
future, but nobody would ever believe her

Castor (*kas*-tor)
one of the famous twins of Greek mythology (Pollux
being the other)

Ceres (*seer*-eez)
goddess of agriculture and especially grain, Ostia's
lifeblood

Cicero (*sis*-sir-row)
famous Roman orator and politician who lived in the
time of Julius Caesar, about a century before this story
takes place

Circus Flaminius (*sir*-kuss fluh-*min*-ee-uss)
racecourse and marketplace opposite the Tiber Island in
Rome

Circus Maximus (*sir*-kuss *max*im-uss)
famous racecourse for chariots, located in Rome,

between the Palatine and Aventine Hills not far from the
Tiber

clepsydra (klep-*see*-dra)

ancient water clock for timing speakers; also a unit of
time (about twenty minutes)

codicil (*kode*-iss-il)

written addition – usually to a will – making a
modification or change

Corinth (kor-inth)

one of the most important cities in the Roman province
of Achaea (Southern Greece), notorious for its lax morals
and beautiful priestesses of Aphrodite

decurion (day-*kyoor*-ee-on)

Ostia's city council was composed of 100 men called
decurions; they had to be freeborn, rich and over
twenty-five years of age

defendant (dee-fen-dant)

person accused in a court of law, opposite of plaintiff

Demosthenes (d'-*moss*-thin-eez)

Greek orator who lived about 400 years before this story
takes place, he was Cicero's great idol and inspiration

Dives (dee-vaze)

a cognomen (surname) which means 'rich' or 'wealthy'

domina (*dom*-in-ah)

Latin word meaning 'mistress'; a polite form of address
for a woman

Domitian (duh-*mish*-un)

son of Vespasian and younger brother to the Emperor
Titus

duovir (doo-*oh*-veer)

one of the two most important magistrates in Ostia, he

served for a year and could preside as the chairman at
trials

ecce! (*ek*-kay)
Latin word meaning 'behold!' or 'look!'

Eleazar (*el*-az-ar)
one of the most famous leaders of the Jewish revolt
against Rome, he died at Masada in AD 73

Ennius (*en*-nee-uss)
author of tragedies, satires and the famous epic *Annales*,
he lived about 300 years before this story

Esquiline (*ess*-kwil-line)
one of the seven hills of Rome, east of the Forum
Romanum

euge! (*oh*-gay)
Latin exclamation meaning 'hurray!'

exordium (ex-*or*-dee-um)
introduction or beginning, especially of a speech

Faunalia (fawn-*al*-ya)
ancient Roman festival of Faunus or Pan; held in the
country rather than the city

Felix (*fee*-licks)
Pollius Felix was a rich patron and poet who lived near
Surrentum

Flavia (*flay*-vee-a)
a name, meaning 'fair-haired'; Flavius is the masculine
form of this name

formula (*for*-myoo-la)
an official statement setting out the legal issues of a case;
it gave the judge authority to declare the defendant guilty
or not guilty

forum (*for*-um)

ancient marketplace and civic centre in Roman towns

garum (*gar*-um)

pungent sauce made of fermented fish entrails, not unlike modern Worcestershire sauce; it was extremely popular among Romans

genius (*jeen*-yuss)

Latin for guardian spirit, usually of the home but also of a person

gladiator (*glad*-ee-ate-or)

man trained to fight other men in the arena, sometimes to the death

gladius (*glad*-ee-uss)

short stabbing sword used by Roman soldiers and some gladiators

Great Revolt (also known as Jewish Revolt against Rome)

began in AD 66 and ended with the destruction of Masada in AD 73

Halicarnassus (hal-ee-car-*nass*-uss)

(modern Bodrum) ancient city in the region of Caria in the Roman province of Asia, it was the site of the famous Mausoleum

haruspex (ha-*roo*-specks)

priest who tells the future by examining entrails of sacrificed animals

Hercules (*her*-kyoo-leez)

very popular Roman demi-god, the equivalent of Greek Herakles

Herod (*hair*-od)

Herod the Great (c.74 BC–c. AD 3) fortified Masada and

built a palace there; he was the Herod who killed the babies of Bethlehem in Matthew's gospel

honestiores (on-ess-tee-*or*-rays)
Roman term for the nobler class of people

humiliores (hyoo-mill-ee-*or*-rays)
the lower classes and those who indulge in shameful occupations like acting

Isola Sacra (eye-*sol*-uh *sack*-ra)
a burial ground in Ostia, north of the Tiber river

Janus (*jan*-uss)
Roman god of doorways and beginnings

Jerusalem (j'-*roo*-sah-lem)
capital of the Roman province of Judaea, it was destroyed in AD 70

Jewish Revolt (also known as Great Revolt against Rome)
began in AD 66 and ended with the destruction of Masada in AD 73

Josephus (jo-*see*-fuss)
Jewish commander who surrendered to Vespasian, became Titus's freedman and wrote *The Jewish War*, an account of the Jewish revolt in seven volumes

Judaea (joo-*dee*-uh)
ancient province of the Roman Empire; part of modern Israel

Juno (*joo*-no)
queen of the Roman gods and wife of the god Jupiter

Jupiter (*joo*-pit-er)
king of the Roman gods, husband of Juno and brother of Pluto and Neptune

jurist

in Roman times 'lawyers' (orators who pleaded a case) and 'judges' (the magistrates who handed down judgement) were ordinary citizens and not experts on the law; when they needed help they went to men who specialised in legal advice: the jurists

kohl (*coal*)

dark powder used to darken eyelids or outline eyes

lararium (lar-*ar*-ee-um)

household shrine, often a chest with a miniature temple on top or a niche in the wall

Laurentum (lore-*ent*-um)

village on the coast of Italy a few miles south of Ostia and site of a villa belonging to Pliny the Younger

lex (lecks)

Latin for 'law', it refers especially to the written law and statutes of Rome

Marcus Antonius (*mar*-kuss an-*tone*-ee-uss)

soldier and statesman who lived during the time of Julius Caesar, a century before this story takes place; he was an enemy of Cicero and had him killed

Marsyas (*mar*-see-ass)

mythological satyr who challenged the god Apollo to a musical contest; when Marsyas lost, his punishment was to be flayed (skinned) alive

Masada (m'-*sah*-duh)

famous Jewish stronghold in the Judean desert near the Dead Sea

Mazal tov (*mah*-zel tav)

Hebrew for 'congratulations'; literally 'good luck'

Medusa (m'-*dyoo*-suh)

mythical female monster with a face so ugly she turned people to stone

Minerva (min-*erv*-uh)

Roman equivalent of Athena, goddess of wisdom, war and weaving

modus operandi (*mo*-duss-op-er-*an*-dee)

Latin for 'way of operating' or 'method of doing something'

mulsum (*mull*-sum)

wine mixed with honey; spices like pepper and saffron were sometimes added

munus (*myoon*-uss)

the Latin word for 'duty' or 'responsibility'

nefas (*neff*-ass)

prohibited, unholy, profane; a dies nefas was a day on which no legal business could be transacted

Neptune (*nep*-tyoon)

god of the sea and also of horses; his Greek equivalent is Poseidon

Nero (*near*-oh)

Emperor who ruled Rome from AD 54-68

Nones (nonz)

7th day of March, May, July, October; 5th day of the others, including December (when this story is set)

Ostia (*oss*-tee-uh)

port about 16 miles southwest of Rome; Ostia is Flavia's home town

Paestum (*pie*-stum)

Greek colony south of the Bay of Naples, site of a Greek temple

palaestra (puh-*lice*-tra)
 exercise area of public baths, usually a sandy courtyard
 open to the sky

palla (*pal*-uh)
 woman's cloak, could also be wrapped round the waist or
 pulled over the head

paterfamilias (*pa*-tare-fa-*mill*-ee-as)
 father or head of the household, with absolute control
 over his children

patina (pa-*teen*-uh)
 Latin for 'dish' or 'pan': a kind of flan with eggs, either
 savoury or sweet

peculium (p'-*kyool*-ee-um)
 gifts or allowance given to a slave by his master or to a
 child-in-power by the paterfamilias; technically, these
 gifts and/or money still belonged to the owner or father

peristyle (*perry*-style)
 a columned walkway around an inner garden or courtyard

peroration (purr-or-*ray*-shun)
 the summing up or conclusion, usually of a speech

persimmon (purr-*sim*-on)
 a soft orange fruit; according to the historian Josephus,
 the Jews burned the persimmon groves around Jerusalem
 to stop the Romans enjoying the fruit

plaintiff (*plane*-tif)
 person who brings suit into a court of law, opposite of
 defendant

plebeian (pleb-*ee*-un)
 from Latin 'plebs'; one of the common people or 'lower

classes', as opposed to those of the equestrian and patrician class

Pliny (*plin*-ee)
now known as Pliny the Younger, Gaius Plinius Secundus was the nephew of Pliny the Elder, who died in the eruption of Vesuvius

Pollux (*pol*-luks)
one of the famous twins of Greek mythology (Castor being the other)

Pontus (*pon*-tuss)
kingdom near the Black Sea, by Flavia's time it was part of the province of Cappodocia

portico (*por*-tik-oh)
roof supported by columns, often attached as a porch or walkway

posca (*poss*-kuh)
well-watered vinegar; a non-alcoholic drink favoured by soldiers on duty

praeco (*pry*-ko)
herald, town crier or auctioneer

praenomen (pry-*no*-men)
the first name of a male Roman citizen, there were only about twenty to choose from

praetor (*pry*-tore)
imperial administrator who often acted as chairman in the law-courts

quadrans (*kwad*-ranz)
small bronze coin worth one sixteenth of a sestertius

Quintilian (kwin-*til*-yun)
Marcus Fabius Quintilianus, c. AD 35-100; great orator

who wrote a treatise on rhetoric called Institutio Oratoria (The Education of an Orator)

rhetor (*ray*-tore)

orator or public speaker, or a teacher of rhetoric

rhetoric (*ret*-or-ik)

the art of persuasive speaking or writing

scroll (skrole)

papyrus or parchment 'book', unrolled from side to side as it was read

sedan chair

mode of conveyance carried by strong men or slaves, like a litter, but the passenger sits instead of reclining

Seneca (*sen*-eh-kuh)

Stoic philosopher who wrote about life and especially about death, he lived from c. BC 4-AD 65

sesterces (sess-*tur*-seez)

more than one *sestertius*, a brass coin; about a day's wage for a labourer

sicarius (sik-*kar*-ee-uss)

type of Jewish assassin who used a curved dagger (sica)

soter (*so*-tare)

Greek word meaning 'saviour'; also used in Latin

stola (*stole*-uh)

a long tunic worn by Roman matrons and respectable women

stylus (*stile*-us)

metal, wood or ivory tool for writing on wax tablets

sub modo (sub *mo*-do)

Latin legal term meaning 'for a special purpose'

Surrentum (sir-*wren*-tum)

modern Sorrento, a harbour town on the Bay of Naples south of Vesuvius

tablinum (tab-*leen*-um)

room in wealthier Roman houses used as the master's study or office, often looking out onto the atrium or inner garden, or both

Tenth Legion

The Legio X Fretensis besieged Jerusalem and Masada during the Jewish Wars of the late first century AD

Tiber (*tie*-bur)

the river that flows through Rome and enters the sea at Ostia

Tiberinus (tie-bur-*ee*-nuss)

deity of the River Tiber; his festival celebrated on 8 December

tiro (*teer*-oh)

novice or beginner

Titus (*tie*-tuss)

Titus Flavius Vespasianus has been Emperor of Rome for a year and a half when this story takes place

triclinium (trik-*lin*-ee-um)

ancient Roman dining room, usually with three couches to recline on

tunic (*tew*-nic)

piece of clothing like a big T-shirt; children often wore a long-sleeved one

usufruct (*yoo*-zoo-frookt)

literally 'using the fruit'; the right to use or sell the fruits of a property without harming or wasting the property itself, eg. eating or selling the harvested grapes without destroying the vines.

vadimonium (va-dim-*oh*-nee-um)

document stating a person's promise to appear at court,

often naming an amount payable if they fail to appear;
like modern bail

Venus (*vee*-nuss)

Roman goddess of love, Aphrodite is her Greek
equivalent

Vespasian (vess-*pay*-zhun)

also known as Titus Flavius Vespasianus, Roman
Emperor who reigned between AD 69–AD 79; he was
the father of Titus and Domitian

Vesta (*vest*-uh)

goddess of the hearth; remains of her temple in Rome can
still be seen today

Vesuvius (vuh-*soov*-yuss)

famous volcano near Naples, which erupted on 24 August
AD 79

Via Ostiensis (*vee*-uh-os-tee-*en*-suss)

the road from Rome to Ostia

vigiles (*vig*-ill-aze)

Roman policemen / firemen; the word literally means
'watchmen'

wax tablet

wax-coated rectangular piece of wood used for making
notes

Zealot (*zel*-ut)

Greek translation of a Hebrew word meaning 'jealous'; in
first century Rome, Zealots were the most militant of the
four main Jewish sects, believing they should oppose
Rome the oppressor by any means, including violence

THE LAST SCROLL

Our legal system and many of our laws originate in ancient Rome. However, ancient Roman law courts were different from today's in many respects. Today, if someone commits a crime, the police arrest him and the state pays a lawyer to prosecute him. In Roman times there was no state prosecutor. A criminal would only be tried if a private individual summoned him to court. People who were not Roman citizens could not file suit; they had to find a patron to do this on their behalf.

Today, lawyers are usually very well paid. In Roman times, lawyers did not receive payment. They were upper-class men who studied rhetoric and then argued cases in order to gain a reputation and advance themselves politically.

Today, witnesses must take an oath, swearing to tell the truth. In Roman times such oaths were optional. Witnesses were often bribed or threatened in order to make them lie. The lawyer himself sometimes insulted and slandered his opponent.

Today, a person on trial will usually try to look his best in court. In Roman times, people would often come to court unwashed and wearing their oldest clothing in order to arouse the sympathy of the judges.

Although all the events and most of the characters in this story are made up, Flaccus, Pliny and Quintilian were real people. Gaius Valerius Flaccus was a high-born poet who would certainly have studied law and rhetoric. Pliny (known today as 'Pliny the Younger') practised law for most of his life and wrote several letters about his experiences in the law courts. Marcus Fabius Quintilianus was a famous teacher of rhetoric. The eleventh volume of his book *Institutio Oratoria* (The Education of an Orator) has lots of practical advice about how to speak and how to do the gestures.

The Jewish stronghold of Masada was taken by the Romans in AD 73. We know from Josephus (*Jewish War* VII. 399ff) that of nearly one thousand defenders, only two women and five children were found alive. It is not known what happened to those seven survivors.